THE
SIREN HUNTER

GEORGE DISMUKES

THE SIREN HUNTER
Copyright © 2023 George Dismukes

ISBN: 979-8-88653-096-4

Melange Books, LLC
White Bear Lake, MN 55110
www.melange-books.com

Published in the United States of America.

Cover Design by Ashley Redbird Designs
Model: Nadine Deffes
Photographer: Helga Schmidt

CHAPTER ONE

Premonition

Angie Holland stood at the railing of the expansive deck on her beach house in San Leon, Texas, staring at nothing in particular. It was early morning. The sun was just beginning to peek over the eastern horizon, revealing a clear blue June sky, and calm water in Dickinson Bay, only a hundred yards distant from Angie's house. Angie had her coffee cup parked on the wide top board of the deck railing.

She brushed her long brown hair back with one hand, and picked up her coffee cup with the other, to take a sip of the hot brew. As she sat the cup down, she peered slightly to her left, to admire the flat water now reflecting the rising sun.

Just at that moment, she heard the patio doors behind her slide open for a moment, then slide closed. She heard the sound of house shoes shuffling across the deck boards toward her. Scott Carrington sidled up beside her with his coffee cup in hand.

"Whaz up?" he asked.

"Nothing. Just enjoying this beautiful, pastoral morning."

"Oh... yeah," Scott said, looking around, obviously still half asleep. Then, "I didn't think you were much of a morning person. This time of day, I usually have to look way deep under the covers to find you."

Angie didn't respond. She was quiet for a very long moment before she said, "It's not over, Scott."

Scott smiled. "Well, I'm glad to hear that, because I plan on loving you forever!"

Angie straightened, turned, and placed her rump against the railing. "Not that! I mean...her. It. The siren thing... It's not over."

Scott, who had been taking a long sip of his coffee, slowly removed the cup from his lips so he could see Angie clearly. "The siren 'thing'? You're not serious? Goddammit, Angie! We all saw her turn into dust right in front of us. Well, anyway, you did. Dust, Angie. Ashes to ashes, dust to dust! She's not coming back. Ding dong, the bitch is gone. The mean ol' wicked bitch is dead!"

Angie looked around, staring at nothing in particular. "I know. I know. But something's bugging me. Something way down, deep inside. I don't know how to explain it. But my instinct tells me there is still a danger. Still, some kind of a threat... I can't explain it."

"You sure it isn't your period?"

"Don't be trite, Scott. No. It's not my period! Why is it, every damned time a woman comes up against a problem, men think it's 'their period'? I think men should have a period. Then, every time they had their tail in a twist about something, a woman could say, 'Is it your period!?'"

"Cheez! Alright. Don't get so upset. I was just asking." Scott eyed Angie for a moment, then turned back toward the patio doors. "Alright. I'm gonna give you your space. You want breakfast?"

"Maybe in a little while," Angie replied.

"Fair enough," Scott said over his shoulder. "I'm going to put biscuits in the oven, if I can figure out how to open that stupid tube without it exploding in my hand and scaring the crap out of me!"

"Courage, corazon mio!" Angie responded. "No guts, no glory! No biscuits, either!"

Angie turned back toward the railing, looked toward the azure blue bay and said softly to herself, "I feel lost. For the first time in my life, I don't know where I am going or what the fuck I'm doing. All I know is something is there, waiting for me. I feel like something is happening to me, inside, and I am frightened that the next step I take will be into a giant, bottomless hole."

It was at that moment that she realized the 'hole' was The Great Blue Hole of Belize.

———

The next morning, Scott Carrington expressed frustration as he drove Angie to the George Bush International Airport to catch a flight to Belize.

"So, if I understand this correctly, you don't know *why* you're going to Belize, all you know is, you've gotta go!"

"I've tried to explain it to you three times now, Scott. You're welcome to come with me."

"I can't. I've got a photo shoot to do down by Kingsville, at the King Ranch.

"Wow! That sounds like an exciting assignment. Well, fly down when you get through with that."

Scott stared straight ahead as he drove down the road, looking frustrated, jaw fixed. "Maybe. Let's see what you've gotten yourself into by then."

"I wish I knew," Angie said.

"If you don't know why you're going there, then why go there? That's the part I don't understand."

"Have you ever had a premonition, Scott? What about those bad dreams that you used to have? Weren't those premonitions?"

Scott thought for a moment. "Yeah.. I guess. Something like that."

"You didn't know what was waiting for you in the Great Blue Hole. You just knew that something was, right?"

"Yeah."

"And the premonitions turned out to be right. It was that bitch from hell, siren."

"Well, we all know how that turned out."

"Okay. Now I know that something is waiting for me. Something without a face. I've got to put a face on it and find out what it is."

"Something tells me I should be alarmed. I'll be down there just as soon as I finish my shoot. Ya know, it sort of pisses me off that you are always right!"

"Sorry! I wish you were going with me now, but I know you have an obligation to fulfill."

"Yep. Gotta keep the wolf away from the front door. He's a hungry bastard!"

"Yes, he is. And now I have to fight with the insurance company because they say we're just inside the hundred-year flood plain, and they want to go up on our insurance to the tune of five thousand dollars a year!"

"Whaaaaat?"

"Don't worry," Angie said as she narrowed her eyes. "I've got Larry the attorney working on it. When people try to screw me, I screw back."

"I know that's right!" Scott said with a half-smile.

CHAPTER TWO

Return to Belize

It took close to two hours to go through all of the inspections, and then wait to be boarded. At last, the plane was in the air and headed south. Only after Angie had ordered a rum & coke did she notice the gent sitting next to her when he said, "Belize, Huh? Your first time there?

Angie turned to look at the older guy who appeared to be in his mid-sixties. Tall, medium build, gray shock of hair, but with piercing blue eyes.

"No," Angie replied. "I've been before."

"First time for me," the older man said, as he accepted his drink from the flight attendant, and nodded thank you to her.

"Really?" Angie said, looking at him. "Diver?"

"What?"

"Diver. Are you a scuba diver?"

"Oh! Oh, no. I'm just trying to get away to some place I've never been before. I don't know why I chose Belize. Just sort of a dart throw."

"What are you running from?" Angie asked, as she took a sip of her rum and coke.

The old man looked at her and smiled an 'almost' smile, then extended his hand. "My name is Richard."

Angie accepted the handshake. "Angie Holland."

"Ah!" Richard exclaimed. "Anglo Saxon. Must have an old heritage from somewhere around England."

"Many generations ago, I suppose. You didn't answer my question. What are you running from?"

Richard chuckled. "A little bit of bulldog in you! Well, the answer is, pain. My wife died recently. She was my closest friend for almost fifty years. Now she's gone on. I miss her every moment of every day... and night. Can't sleep without waking up in a cold sweat. I just need to find some direction, a reason to keep on living. So far, I haven't done that. I doubt that I'll find my answer in Belize, but maybe I can make myself distracted enough that I will forget, for a blessed moment. I need some rest, badly!"

"I'm very sorry. What was her name?"

"Angela. Just like the angels."

Angie fell silent for several minutes, digesting Richard's words. Finally, she said, "If you aren't going there to dive, where are you going in Belize?"

"I don't really know," Richard answered. "I have thought about going out to that little island they call Ambergris Caye. I understand they have nice accommodations there. You? Where are you going?"

"A place south of Belize City, well, actually, in the extreme southern part of the country, on the coast. The little town is called Placencia. The resort is called Robert's Grove Resort. I like it there."

This started a conversation about Robert's Grove that lasted several minutes. By the time the plane landed in Belize, Richard had changed his mind and decided he wanted to accompany Angie to Placencia, and Robert's Grove.

At Belize International, Angie & Richard cleared customs, then walked to the opposite side of the airport to catch an Island Hopper to Placencia.

When they landed at Placencia, they climbed aboard a Robert's Grove limo, which was there to collect guests with reservations at Robert's Grove Resort. Once they had arrived at the resort, helpers were waiting to grab their baggage and carry it into the reception area. Dr. Maurine Howard was behind the reception desk, fiddling with some paperwork. When she looked up and saw Angie, she was surprised.

"Angie! What in the world? You should have told me you were coming! I could have had my best room ready for you. Who's your friend?"

"His name is Richard," Angie said as she took the tote bag off of her shoulder. "We met on the plane. He was gonna go out to Ambergris Caye. I changed his mind, brought you a customer.

Maurine extended her hand to Richard. "Maurine Howard," she said.

"Richard Hart," Richard responded with a smile.

"So, what brings you to Belize?" Maurine asked.

"Uh, a search."

"Oh! What are you searching for?" Maurine asked.

"Me!" Richard responded. "My wife passed a few

months ago, and I have lost me, somewhere along the way. Maybe that's because so much of me was her."

"Oh dear!" Maurine exclaimed. "I'm sorry for your loss... and your pain. I'm not sure what all we can do to help, but let's begin with a couple of Siren's Potions to welcome you. Then we'll take it from there."

Maurine led the way to the nearest of two bars at Robert's Grove. Richard followed Maurine, saying, "Siren's Potion?" At Maurine's side was a small champagne colored dog named Dolly. It was long haired and most likely a mixed breed with chihuahua Dachshund and terrier in it.

"It's a long story!" Angie said, sandwiching in between Maurine and Richard, going out the door of the reception area.

———

On the deck, at the beachside bar, the trio settled into comfortable chairs. Angie whistled to Dolly, who jumped up in her lap. Then Angie and Richard began sipping on their Siren's Potion drinks. Maurine stuck with a lemonade, for now.

Richard looked at his glass appreciably. "Siren's Potion, eh? This is pretty good stuff. But something tells me it will take me a mile or so beyond where I want to go."

"That is a definite possibility," Maurine admonished. "Enjoy but take it slow!" Then, "So, tell me, Angie, what brings you to our happy resort so suddenly, and by that I mean, without warning?"

Angie hesitated. "Following my instinct. A premonition."

Maurine eyed Angie. "Oh no! You don't think…"

"I don't know what to think," Angie confessed. "*Something* told me to come down here. So, I'm here."

"Oh my God!" Maurine gasped, a worried expression coming across her face. "I thought it was over!"

As the trio chatted, they failed to notice the exotic looking woman, a hundred yards away, on the beach in a blue bikini. The woman stared at them intently, without moving for several long moments, through eyes that were almond shaped and with elliptical pupils. She was clearly unworldly. Then she waded into the water, dove beneath the surface, but never resurfaced.

Meanwhile, on the deck, Richard squinted and wrinkled his brow in curiosity. "Somebody want to fill me in on the missing parts?" Richard asked.

"It *is* over. At least, I think it is," Angie said, ignoring Richard for the moment. "This might be something else altogether.

"Well, I hope so. This place is just getting back to normal after that circus last year."

"Excuse me," Richard complained. "It's obvious that I have parachuted into the middle of a long standing something or other. But my curiosity has got me twisting my eyebrows out of shape. So, can I *please*, know the rest of the story, as Paul Harvey would say?"

"The siren," Maurine said, offhandedly.

"Siren?" Richard looked more puzzled than ever.

"It's a long story," Angie said.

"They killed her, there beside the dock last year," Maurine added.

Richard looked shocked. "Killed her? You said, 'Killed her!'"

"Had to be done," Maurine said, matter of factly.

"There's no telling how many people she would have slaughtered," Angie added.

Richard turned his glass up and drank the contents. "I need another Siren's Potion," he said, wiping his mouth. "Maybe a whole bucket full of them!"

Angie and Maurine looked at Richard, expressionless, then looked at one another and smiled. Maurine then signaled to Oscar, the bartender, to refill both glasses, and to give her a Siren's Potion as well.

The next hour and a half were spent filling in the blanks for Richard Hart, who, as it turned out, was a very likable person. Nevertheless, his expressions were a kaleidoscope, ranging from surprise, to shock, to disbelief as he listened to every word that dropped from the ladies' mouths like rain. When they had reached the end of their tale, Richard was wide eyed, and staring out at the beach with awe.

"I have to be honest," Richard said. "I would think you were both ready for a rubber room except that I vaguely remember all the hubbub on TV about the boat load of missing divers. I just never connected that story with 'here.' Now, here I am! I find myself at the very place where the end played out."

"Well, we hope it was the end," Angie added, looking uncertain.

"What do you mean by that?" Richard asked.

"I wish I knew," Angie said, looking at nothing in particular. "I wish I knew."

CHAPTER THREE

A Certification & A Celebration

When Angie entered the restaurant the next morning, she found Richard Hart there, sitting at a table near a window, with bloodshot eyes, sipping on a Bloody Mary. Angie plopped down in the chair across from him and pointed to his Bloody Mary when a waiter approached the table.

"I need one of those," she said with a half-smile.

"Right away, Miss," the waiter said, and retreated.

"I would ask how you're doing, but I think I can guess," she said.

"My head feels like an old tennis shoe that somebody left in the dryer," Richard said. "It was enough, getting swacked on my first night here, but I didn't sleep much, trying to wrap my head around everything you ladies revealed to me last night."

"Well, you asked," Angie said, as the waiter arrived with her Bloody Mary.

"Yes, I did," Richard conceded. "But I had no idea what a can of worms I was opening."

"You know the old saying; be careful what you ask for…"

"Yes, but it isn't quite that simple, is it? Correct me if I'm wrong, but a synopsis of this is, you came down here on a yacht safari a couple of years ago and encountered a woman, or maybe a being, that you concluded was a mythological creature."

"Correct."

"A two-thousand-year-old offspring of a siren. But she had the ability to appear to everyone who saw her as a beautiful woman, even to the extent of appearing a different age and attributes to each, according to that person's fantasy vision of beauty."

"Yep."

"So, you killed her. Or at least someone in your party did. A pre-pubescent young man named James?"

"You're doing good so far."

"But then, as it turned out, the attempt to dispatch this evil being failed, somehow. Or, to put it in your words, 'Ding dong, the bitch ain't dead.'"

"Right again."

"Okay, I'm batting a thousand. Now, to continue… a year later, you saw a news program on TV, reporting that several people were missing who had been aboard a different yacht at The Great Blue Hole."

Angie nodded agreement.

"So, that was the starting gun of a whole new chapter in this ongoing saga. You, along with other members of your posse, wound up back down here on a mission to seek and destroy the same creature from Mythology as you 'thought' you had done-in previously. Only this time, you received instructions from *other creatures,* also from Mythology, who told you how to cook the siren's goose.

"This involved, 'among other things,' the necessity of the siren, the very thing you were trying to kill, to murder another innocent victim at the precise same time she was being stabbed to death with a special dagger? One made of... what was it? Obsolete..?"

"Obsidian," Angie corrected.

"Sorry, yes, obsidian. Have I left anything out?"

"Quite a bit. Part of the recipe was that she had to be emotionally weakened, crippled, as it were, compromised by being in love and hurting from that. She was in disguise as another person, a young woman whom she named Mara. And once again, the person who dispatched her had to be pre-pubescent."

Richard sat back in his chair and blinked. He also made a soft whistling sound. "Well, you know what? I guess I believe you because I don't think anybody could just make this stuff up! It's an incredible story, and if you actually lived it, it's a one-of-a-kind adventure beyond compare!"

At that moment, Maurine, accompanied by Dolly, approached the table, carrying a handful of 8" x 10" photographs. "May I join you?" she said as she sat down. "I overheard part of what you were saying, so I went to my office and got these. They're pictures of some of the circus that was going on at the time. That one is of a sea creature some divers speared out at the Blue Hole, which was assumed to be Maris's father," she said, handing the photograph to Richard.

Richard looked at the photo for several long moments.

"Father? This ugly sonofabitch was the father? Father of a beautiful temptress? The voluptuous, siren?"

"Well," Angie said with a half-smile, "she wasn't all that much to look at when she wasn't morphed as a woman!"

Richard looked up from the pictures to Angie, then to Maurine, who sat silent, holding a sheaf of more pictures. "Ladies, I'm approaching overload here," Richard said incredulously. "This would be far out enough if it was a Grimm's Fairy Tale! But you're telling it as truth, and now you're supporting the story with photographic evidence. May I see those other pictures?"

Richard accepted the pictures from Maurine and began looking through them slowly, spending as much as a minute on each one, often with Maurine explaining the scene that was captured.

"This one is of various news people at a briefing right here on the deck. It looks different because there were so many people here."

After Richard had carefully inspected all of the photographs, he emptied his Bloody Mary and signaled for the waiter. "Would you care for a refill, Angie? Maurine, can I offer you an early morning pick me up?"

"Actually, I think I'll have a Virgin Mary," Maurine said, half to the waiter who had just arrived. Having the drink orders, the waiter retreated.

Richard turned back to Angie. "So, the 'up to the moment' news update is that you felt some strange premonition, a 'magnetism' that inspired you to come back down here? You feel there is still 'something' waiting for you? Something 'unfinished' as it were?"

"That's about the size of it, yeah," Angie confirmed.

Richard sat back in his chair with a strange look on his face. "Ohhh, this has just got to be good! I want to be a part of whatever's coming! I'm sticking around! So, what's next?"

"I'm not sure," Angie said. "Maybe nothing. I'll know it when I see it, or when I feel it."

"Until then?"

"I will wait, act like I'm on vacation. Go swimming, walk on the beach. Maybe even go out to The Great Blue Hole to see what I can find."

"Okay. I can... I'd like to hire on as your bodyguard. That will give me all the reason I need to be around when whatever it is happens."

"Bodyguard? I don't know how much good that will do. Besides, what do you know about being a bodyguard?

"I owned a security company for thirty years. I think I can handle it."

"Fair enough. But know this, you might be biting off more than you can chew. These creatures aren't like stopping some crazy weirdo who tries to pull a gun on the president. They will send you to hell, and then eat an ice cream cone."

Richard nodded agreement and smiled. "I get it. It's not a problem. If I got killed tomorrow, I would be ready. My wife, Angela, is waiting for me. I know she is. So, I'm not afraid to cross over. I've lived my life here. You, on the other hand, are probably the bravest woman I have ever met."

Angie and Maurine stared at Richard. He even offered a wane smile when he finished his statement. To the ladies, it almost sounded like he wanted to 'go'.

Maurine ordered a breakfast banquet for the three of them. Not only was it just for fun, but the good Doctor Maurine also thought a breakfast feast might somehow alter the mood. She also had the chef prepare plain scrambled eggs sans salt or pepper, for Dolly.

The first thing to arrive was a huge bowl with a selection of several exotic fruits, including banana, pineapple, mango, papaya, cantaloupe and citrus, with lots of sectioned key limes to squeeze on the fruits. The second course comprised of delicious link sausages and eggs, some deviled, some over easy, served with a slightly hotter than mild salsa. To drink, there was ample hot coffee, certainly enough to chase any hangover.

During the breakfast yik-yak, Angie said, "I'm thinking of doing a day trip to the Blue Hole."

"Why would you want to go there?" Maurine asked.

"The obvious place to begin a serious search," Angie replied, while munching on a slice of rich mango. "I want to see what kind of 'vibes' I pick up there."

"Do you want to dive the hole?"

"Yeah, but I don't have a dive buddy. I'm not about to go down in that place alone. You know any divers around here that might want to go with me?"

"What about me?" Richard asked.

"You said you aren't a diver?" Angie said.

"No. But I'm a fast learner.

Angie wiped her mouth with a white cloth napkin. "It's not all that easy. You have to be certified, and Maurine here would be unable, by law, to rent you equipment without seeing your 'C' card."

Richard smiled as he stabbed at a sausage. "So, what do I do to get certified?"

"How old are you?" Maurine asked.

"Sixty-five," Richard said, almost proudly.

Maurine nodded. "The first thing we would have to do is call the doc and get you a physical exam. After that, providing the doctor gives the okay, I have an instructor. You would have to pay him and take a crash course. It's called a 'resort' course. He might be able to cram it into a week. Then, you would have to do shallow check-out dives. After that, you can graduate. But unless you are in really good health, I would still advise against such a deep dive. The place Angie is talking about is 150 feet, straight down. It's a dive for advanced, seasoned divers."

Richard smiled. It was plain that he dismissed some of what Maurine had said, because like all aging men, in his mind and heart, he could still do anything. "Let's get started!" he said, excitement in his voice. "Call that saw bones and make an appointment for me, please."

Maurine looked at Angie. Angie motioned by holding her hands, palms up. Maurine picked up her cell phone and made the call.

———

Later that afternoon, Dr. Clarence Smith, Placencia's most renowned MD, walked into the office area of Robert's Grove, and sat down in a chair across from Dr. Maurine Howard and Dolly.

"He's one of the most fit men for his age that I have ever examined. No major surgeries, no stints, no strokes. He's not on any kind of medication. I drew blood for blood-work, but that won't be back for a few days. I would have to say, if he wants to take resort scuba training, let him do it. The results of his blood work will be back before he finishes. If I find something unusual, there's time to let you know before he's certified."

Maurine thanked the doctor, then went to find Richard Hart with Dolly at her side and give him the news. She also put in a call to her scuba instructor and told him that she had a new student for him.

She found Richard, wearing a tropical, Hawaiian style blue shirt, white shorts, and a straw hat, standing on the beach, looking out at the water. He seemed to be deep in thought. Maurine approached him with a smile. "Good afternoon!" she said.

Richard turned his head to see who it was. "Oh! Hi! Good afternoon."

"You are cleared to begin scuba training. I have a man named Oscar on his way over here to sign you up and get you started."

"Really? Thank you. I appreciate that." Then he resumed staring at the ocean, as if he was far away.

"Beautiful, isn't it?" Maurine said.

"Angela would have loved it here," Richard replied. "Even when we started getting older, there was always something young, and untamed about her. She was a born adventurer."

Maurine thought about that. "I'm sorry for your loss. It's obvious that you loved her very much.

"She was my sunrise and my sunset. She was the beat of my heart. The keeper of my dreams.

Maurine said nothing. She just stood beside Richard, looking at him.

"Richard wiped away a tear. "It seems like just yesterday that we were married. I don't know what happened. One day we were twenty-five. The next day we were in our sixties. Time is a merciless, damnable bastard thing that melts between your fingers."

"It is that!" Maurine agreed.

Richard finally turned away from the water. "So, what else are you up to this afternoon?" he asked with a smile.

"I have a resort to run," Maurine said. "Making sure that people are care-free and have fun is a full-time job."

Richard started walking slowly down the beach. The natural thing for Maurine seemed to do was to join him.

"Interesting big black birds you have here," he said, pointing up. "They seem to enjoy just hanging on air currents and behaving like living kites. I like the big scissor tails."

"They're called frigate birds," Maurine said, looking up.

"Frigate birds!" Richard repeated. "Interesting. Guess I didn't travel enough. There's a lot of things I missed. I lived sort of a cookie cutter life. The kind you see in Norman Rockwell paintings. I ran a business, tried to be thoughtful about the amount of time I spent at home; but still, when you own your own business, you always spend more time than you should at the office. When we managed to get away for vacations, it was to places like Niagara Falls, or The Grand Canyon. Angela liked going to Las Vegas a lot. Not just for the gambling, but the shows. What about you? How did you wind up here, in Belize, owning a business?"

"I'm afraid that's a long and winding road," Maurine

said, looking out at the water. "I need to be about half in the bag before I get loose enough to tell that story. But it started with my love of it down here. The tropical breezes, the laid-back attitude of people, the exotic food."

Richard chuckled. "Well, now I have a goal! I'll have to make it my mission to get you 'half in the bag'."

"That might be fun," Maurine admitted. "But right now, you'll have to excuse me. I have to get back to that business we were mentioning."

Maurine parted ways with Richard, but not before patting him on the shoulder, then walked back toward the office, Dolly at her side. Her direction of travel was toward her office, but her thoughts were still with Richard. There was something about him that touched her where she hadn't been touched in a long time. Something a little too close to the heart.

Maybe it was the fact that he was so different from that drunk SOB she had been married to in Houston. Drunk, narcissist bastard! The marriage had only lasted three years. Three years longer than it should have! She had dumped his ass and never looked back.

Richard's memories were of someone he adored. Maurine's memories were of someone who ignored her, except when he was verbally abusing her. The rest of the time, he had a mistress that lived in a bottle. How many times had she seen him, passed out drunk on the sofa? ... Enough! She didn't want to go there in her mind. Besides, there were things to tend to in the here and now. That old saying popped into her head as a life preserver: "The reason a rear-view mirror is so much smaller than a windshield is because you are supposed to spend more time looking ahead than looking back!" It is a good philosophy, and a good policy. But she did allow herself to wonder, fleetingly, why there weren't more men like Richard!

Oscar Villereal was arriving just as she walked into her office. She halted long enough to greet him and say, "Your new student is named Richard Hart. I just left him. He's walking down at the beach, wearing a blue shirt and a straw hat. I think you'll like him. He's sixty-five, but the doc has checked him out, so he's clear to go."

"Thank you, Dr. Maurine," Oscar said, and walked away toward the beach.

Once back at her desk, she shuffled a few papers, but couldn't concentrate, so left the office to go look for Angie.

There were several resort guests lounging on the deck beside the pool. She greeted each one of them with a smile and a hello, stopping one time to ask if there was something a lady needed. She finally spotted Angie, standing on the far end of the deck, watching Oscar and Richard, who were in conversation on the beach, fifty yards away.

"I think Oscar is getting your friend Richard signed up. If I know Oscar, he'll probably begin lessons today," Maurine said as she approached Angie.

"That's good," Angie said. "I wish he was already certi-fied. I'm anxious to get on out to the hole."

"So now it isn't a 'maybe'. You've made your mind up? Well, just chill for a few days. Something tells me you need it. You seem very up tight."

"Up tight?" Angie repeated. "I'm tighter than a fucking violin string, and I don't know why. Something is just... 'there'. It's pestering me and won't leave me alone. I don't know what it is, Maurine. And if it has to do with that damned siren, I don't know *why* it's me. Why me? Why am I here? I've never been so confused in my life.

"Life used to be simple, you know. I got up in the morning. I knew what I was supposed to do, and I did it. I'm good at it. I'm a businesswoman. I make money. I *like* to make money. It's fun! It's natural. Then, all of this crap started with Scott's dreams. That led to an unbelievable chapter in my life, where people got killed, including the siren, or so we thought. The next thing I knew, my focus got altered again, without me having anything to say about it. I became an unintentional pawn, a siren hunter. More people got killed, and the same damned siren was involved who we thought we had already put out of her fucking misery.

"So, okay, it's finally over! Life can get back to normal, right? Wrong! Here I am a third time. Only this time, I don't have a clue what's supposed to happen or how. I just know that it is here. Right fucking here! So, here I am, standing around with my thumb in my ear, waiting for the other shoe to drop. It's not a good feeling."

Maurine had been watching Angie rant for the past minute or so. So finally, she suggested, "Angie, I think the reason you are here is because you have been chosen by something or somebody, who knows a lot more than you or I. I think they know that you are the only person who can do whatever needs to be done...confront whatever needs to be confronted, and deal with it. You, with your very special, unique talents."

"You mean, to confront the person or thing that I am supposed to confront?"

"Exactly. Why would they want you here? If, as you suspect, this person or thing knows you are a threat to its existence, why would *it* summon you here? That 'thing' didn't summon you. Something celestial did."

"Hmmm. You know, what you say makes sense. Maybe a little too much sense. You are a very wise woman, Maurine. That gives me a whole different perspective on this. Thank you!"

"You're welcome. Now, why don't you go change into a swimsuit and take advantage of that swimming pool over there. I can also have the waiter bring you something a little less potent than a Siren's Potion."

"Sounds like a plan. Let's face it, I'm in park mode anyway, until Richard completes his scuba stuff."

"Well put. Let me go talk to the bartender."

Angie walked toward her room, flanked by Maurine and Dolly, until they reached the restaurant door, where Maurine and Dolly turned to the left. Angie went straight.

———

Richard Hart attacked scuba training like a hungry dog goes after a sweet biscuit. He absorbed the classroom information almost faster than Oscar Villereal could give it. In the pool, he went through every aspect practice as if he had been a diver for years. In record time, Oscar had his new student on a boat, going out, away from shore a few hundred yards to a place just inside the Great Barrier Reef of Belize, where the water is only thirty feet deep, to do his check-out dives. Richard easily passed. He was a natural scuba diver.

On a Friday night, four people held a small party and a ceremony, where Oscar Villereal ceremoniously presented

Richard Hart with his certification card. Present were Angie, Maurine, Oscar and Richard Hart. Richard was now a certified diver.

"Under normal circumstances, I would recommend several deep dives down to seventy, or eighty feet before attempting anything like the Blue Hole," Oscar admonished. "But if there is one thing I have learned about you, Richard, it is that you are unstoppable. So, do what you have to do, and watch that decompression stop on the way back up very closely.

"Better yet, I book charters to the hole, so I will take you out there when you are ready to go, and also serve as your dive master." Looking at Angie, Oscar smiled and said, "I will be with you, to make sure no accidents happen. So, there will be three of us diving. And that is actually the way it is supposed to be, anyway."

"Agreed!" Richard Hart said with a smile and extended his hand for a handshake with his instructor. "Oscar, my man, it's been a pleasure working with you. Thank you for being so thorough. I feel like I have learned a lot in the past few days! Now, let's celebrate!"

And celebrate they did! They ate every form of seafood to be found in the area; Robalo (snook), Caribbean king crab, lobster, shrimp, and washed it all down with white wine. It was Richard's graduation, and Richard's treat. So, he wanted no boundaries. Several other guests that wandered into the restaurant were invited to "Partake of the Manna of The Gods," as Richard put it. And despite the fact that Richard drank quite a bit, he maintained his composure. He continued to be friendly, happy and articulate. When he reached a certain point, he cut himself off from drinking alcohol and switched to hot tea.

This was as surprising as it was pleasing to Maurine, who had lived for years with a man who didn't have the sense to stop at any point. She had been watching Richard closely for the tell-tale signs of an alcoholic. They weren't there. Her relief could be measured with a yard stick.

Quite to the contrary, Richard seemed to pull in his own horns, without help, and return to a calmer, more logical demeanor. "This has been a wonderful celebration," he said. "And I am really psyched about being a certified scuba diver. But I am also glad that I won't be the one who has to clean up this mess!" He looked around at the remains of the feast.

He turned to Maurine. "Would you ask our two waiters to come here for a moment, please?"

"Sure," she said, and motioned for the waiters. When they arrived, Richard reached in his pocket and unwrapped two, one-hundred-dollar bills from a wad of money bound with a money clip. He handed each one of the waiters a bill. "Gentlemen, I want to thank you for taking such good care of us here, tonight. I know we have been a mess and made a mess. I hope this will compensate for your patience and also make clean up a little less painless." The waiters both thanked him and retreated to a respectful distance, ready to attend to whatever needs their special diners needed.

When everybody got up to leave, Maurine said, "That was very nice of you, Richard. Thank you. I know those boys both have families. The extra money will be a blessing to them."

"My pleasure," Richard said, and started to say something else when Oscar came up behind them.

"Excuse me," Oscar said. "The Great Blue Hole is a deep dive, and a dangerous one. I recommend that we chill and recover tomorrow. Drink no alcohol at all. Then, we will go to the hole on Sunday. Eh? Does that sound alright with everybody?"

"It sounds very responsible to me," Richard said. "Sunday it is!"

"Sunday!" Angie said and walked toward her room. Maurine retreated to her quarters, Dolly faithfully in tow. And from the dark surface of the water in the marina, only yards away, two eyes watched intently, unblinking, from inches above the surface.

———

Saturday was the designated R & R day, used to recuperate from the 'graduation ceremony'. Maurine encouraged fresh squeezed fruit juice, which included, primarily, guava juice. But also, plenty of orange juice and grapefruit, with a vitamin filled liquado (smoothie) made from banana and mango. Richard swam laps in the pool while Maurine looked on every chance she got, in between performing her duties as a resort owner and operator.

Angie walked on the beach. Something was eating at her nonstop. And there seemed to be nothing Maurine, or anybody else could do to help.

Scott called at one point. "I'm here, on the King Ranch. It's amazing! I just saw a fucking indigo snake that had to be close to ten feet long. It was beautiful! There are wild, white-tailed deer running around here in thick herds. Wild deer... in herds! And the cattle! They showed me a bull with nuts the size of basketballs!"

"Thank you so much for that report! Deer, big snakes and bovines with giant testicles, oh my!" Angie said, smiling.

"So, what's going on there?"

"Not much, so far. But it's coming. I can feel it. Say Scott, do you remember Al Harmon's friend who came down here with the obsidian dagger?"

"I remember him. I don't remember his name."

"Well, how about calling Al. Tell him we need to borrow that dagger again. See if you can bring it when you come down here."

"Oh shit! Alright, I'll see what I can do."

"Oh shit? Don't fail me, Scott. We're going to need it." With that closing thought, Angie ended the call.

CHAPTER FOUR

Return To the Great Blue Hole

At the crack of dawn on Sunday, Oscar Villereal had all preparations made for a day trip to The Great Blue Hole. The thirty-four-foot Sea Ray, named, BELIZE WHAT YOU WANT, was topped off with fuel. Ample food and drinks were on board, a rack of filled aluminum 80 air tanks had all been checked for proper fill pressure and locked in place, everything down to sunscreen and extra pairs of sunglasses were on hand.

Angie and Richard came walking down the dock toward the boat exactly on time, carrying their scuba equipment bags, plus one extra item. Angie carried a five-foot-long bang-stick in her left hand.

"What is that for?" Oscar asked, as Angie climbed on board.

"Sharks," Angie responded to Oscar as she stepped into the boat.

"Morning!" Richard said, as he followed Angie onto the dive boat.

"Good morning to both of you," Oscar replied,

accepting their dive bags and passing them across to Henry Ochoa, the deckhand.

While Henry stowed the gear bags, Oscar started the engines, which thundered to life in the early morning calm. Henry spryly hopped onto the pier, freed the lines from the chocks and then jumped back onto the boat. Thus unencumbered, Oscar inched the Belize What You Want, away from the pier. When it was clear of the structure, he pointed the craft toward the lagoon. From there, it would be about a forty-five-minute trip, just to get to open water. Then another hour to the Blue Hole. If they would have looked back, they would have seen Maurine standing at the railing on the dock in front of the Habanero Restaurant, watching them depart.

———

About two hours later, they approached Lighthouse Reef, and Oscar slowed the Belize What You Want to a crawl as he negotiated his way through shallow coral heads. When at last Oscar cleared the last coral head and entered The Great Blue Hole proper, he steered the boat out over the middle of the hole so that everyone could get a good look down into the water.

"Wow!" Richard said. "I've never seen water this clear. It's like looking into liquid air! Is that the bottom, down there where that white stuff is?"

"No," Oscar replied. "That is a thermocline. It's about ten feet thick, and we are going to have to drop down through it. While we are in 'the cloud', you won't be able to see your hand in front of your face. Then, when you come out on the bottom side of it, the light is going to be dim, and you're going to be face to face with those grottos. The best word to describe them is 'spooky.' Also, remember me telling you about Martini's Law? You'll be at a three-martini depth, so it will be easy to become confused, or paranoid. Go slow and carefully think through anything that you do."

Oscar piloted the boat back toward the edge of the hole, so that Henry could toss an anchor between coral heads and secure the boat before Oscar killed the motors. It seemed blissfully quiet after listening to the drone of the motors for two hours.

Then, gearing up began. All three divers worried themselves into wet suits, often with the assistance of Henry Ochoa. Then came the weight belts, and BCs with air tanks and regulators attached, which had to be gotten into, and finally fins and masks. After each diver checked to make sure they had the right pressure in their tanks, it was time to go overboard. Oscar's last order to Henry before everyone went into the water was, "Make very sure those decompression stop tanks are waiting at the right depth."

"No problem," Henry assured his boss. Then, at Oscar's signal, all three divers fell backwards into the water. After checking to make sure their regulators were working properly, and purging their BCs of all air, they did the diver's roll over in the water, and descended. The sandy slope was only a few feet below them. That slope dropped at a 25-degree angle for about thirty feet, until it reached the rim of the Blue Hole. There, the bottom fell away. There was a sheer, vertical wall that went straight down four hundred and eight feet to a bottom, cluttered with remnants of what was once a ceiling over this phenomenon when it was a cave, above water. But that had been over fifty thousand years ago. When the last ice age thawed, and the water level began to rise. The water rose high enough to swallow the entire reef, and this cave became an underwater labyrinth.

The three divers fell effortlessly, and in slow motion, down the side of the vertical stone wall. The water here is so clear, one has a tendency to be a little frightened of falling.

They approached the thermocline, entered it, and just as Oscar had warned, visibility was immediately reduced to zero. Richard had to suppress panic, because here, he could not rate his speed of descent. He was in limbo, vulnerable to anything that might want to attack him. He was completely defenseless.

A moment later, they emerged on the bottom side of the thermocline and all three divers sighed relief. But now, they were in a seeming different world. The light here was one half of what it was above the thermocline, which created an eerie feeling. Also at this depth, all colors were filtered out by the water, making everything look blue or black. The only way to discover the true color of something was to shine a flashlight on it.

They continued their slow-motion free fall, until they came face to face with huge openings in the wall that were filled with ghastly looking mineral formations, stalactites, and stalagmites, which made the caves look like giant opened fang filled maws, ready to bite down on anything that entered.

Oscar had been on target when he explained the effects of Martini's Law. Richard felt inebriated, and because of the sensation, it would have been easy to hallucinate and imagine the mineral formations being alive and blood thirsty. He found himself using words he hadn't used in years to fight back the fear. This was, after all, a limestone phenomenon. Inanimate, an underwater prisoner for thousands of years. Lifeless, emotionless, a frozen spectacle here for his amazement. And also, hidden in complete darkness until a few years ago.

It seemed that they had barely arrived at the grottos when Oscar banged his dive knife against his scuba tank and gave the five-minute signal. Richard swallowed his apprehension and moved forward, slightly into the grotto, so he could touch a huge hanging stalactite, and by doing so, conquer it. Better yet, if he could get Oscar to take his picture while touching it, so he would have evidence. Angie quickly joined him on the opposite side on the stalactite, placing her gloved hand against it, and turning toward Oscar for a picture. Oscar accommodated their wish. The flash on his camera went off, confirming the photo.

Then, because of Richard's age, the group "cut five" off of their bottom time, and slowly headed to the surface. Richard was ecstatic! This underwater adventure was something not only new to him, but foreign from anything he had ever known. He wanted to yell 'Yahoo', but of course, could not while he was under water!

Upward, back through the thermocline they went, only this time, they were not falling, they were ascending. So, Richard really poured on the coal with his flippers, not wanting to be in the white milk any longer than necessary. When he emerged above it, his relief was obvious. He looked up and even though they were over one hundred feet under the water, he could plainly see the outline of the hull of the boat, and the decompression tanks hanging on the end of a line.

All three divers swam up to where the decompression tanks were suspended in the water. They carefully checked their depth gauge to make sure they were no shallower than ten feet, then held onto the tanks and switched to the regulators that were provided there. They outgassed for ten minutes, then traveled on to the surface.

Where was Henry? Oscar was surprised that he was not waiting for them when they surfaced at the stern of the boat. He was supposed to be standing on the dive platform to help the divers out of the water. He would accept the swim fins as they were removed and handed to him, toss them into the stern of the boat, then help each diver up the ladder, usually by grabbing the top of the BC and lifting it, to take the weight of the air tank off of the diver.

That's how things were 'supposed' to go. But Henry wasn't waiting on the dive platform. Was he preoccupied, doing something else? Maybe he was on that damned cell phone of his and lost track of time?

Oscar was the first one out of the water. Therefore, he did the job that Henry was supposed to do. But while he was assisting Angie, and then Richard, out of the water, he was calling for Henry.

"Henry? Where the fuck are you? Get back here and do your job! This is what I pay you for, not to talk to guapas (cute girls) on that frigging phone!"

When there was no response, Oscar started to get irritated. He climbed the short ladder up into the stern of the boat and went to the hatch, leading to the cabin. If that little bastard was napping, Oscar was going to fire him. Instead, on the way to the hatch Oscar stepped on something that was a little sticky. He looked down to see what it was and saw dark red spots. Blood? There were several large drops of it on the stern deck. But there was no sign of Henry, anywhere.

"What the hell?" Oscar said and began searching all areas of the boat. At first, he thought Henry might have cut himself somehow, and went below to find the First Aid kit. But he was nowhere on the boat. Alarmed, Oscar then visually searched the perimeter around the vessel. That's when a dread set in that something had happened to his deckhand. He stood on the bow of the boat, searching desperately, with binoculars, looking among the coral heads. Although he didn't know why, for to search there didn't make any sense.

After several minutes of his visual search sans results, he said, "It's time to call the Coast Guard. Something is terribly wrong!" He worked his way to the pilot area of the boat and grabbed the microphone of his ship-to-shore radio.

"Mayday, Mayday. This is the pleasure craft, Belize What You Want. We are at The Great Blue Hole, and we are missing a man. He is nowhere to be found... has just disappeared."

It only took a moment for a voice to come back over his radio. "This is Belize Sea Rescue. How long has your man been missing?"

"Less than an hour," Oscar answered into the microphone. "He is my deckhand. We went diving. When we came back up, he was gone. There's a few drops of blood on the stern deck, but nothing else."

"We are on the way," the voice came back. That communication-initiated radio traffic from several different origins, including the Belize Coast Guard. The Great Blue Hole was about the become a very busy place.

Among other calls received on the ship-to-shore radio, was one from Dr. Maurine Howard. "Robert's Grove Resort, calling Pleasure Craft Belize What You Want."

Oscar was standing by the radio, microphone in hand. "Hey, Dr. Maurine!"

"What's going on out there?" she asked.

"Henry is missing," Oscar replied, worry now evident in his voice.

"Missing?" Maurine said. "That doesn't make any sense. How did he go missing?"

"I went diving to the grottos with Miss Holland and Richard. When we left the boat, Henry was here. When we surfaced, several minutes later, he was gone. There are some drops of blood on the stern deck that are very concerning. There is nothing else."

"Oh, my God!" Maurine said. "Is Angie there?"

"Of course. She's right here. You want to talk to her?"

"Yes."

Oscar handed Angie the microphone and stepped out of the way. "Hey, Maurine," Angie said.

"Something tells me your 'down deep feelings' may have been on target."

"It sure is starting to look that way."

"That's the same thing that happened to that boat load of divers the last time."

"Practically a carbon copy. But it can't be Maris. It just

can't be. I saw her turn into a burnt marshmallow right in front of me. There was nothing left but a pile of ashes."

"Then who? Or what?"

"I don't know. I have some suspicions, but I don't want to talk about them over the radio. Too many ears."

"I understand," Maurine said. Then, "How is Richard doing?"

Angie looked at Richard, only a few feet away. "He's handling it well, so far. You want to talk to him?"

"Yes, please."

Richard stepped close to the radio. Angie handed him the microphone and stepped out of the way. Richard pressed the talk button. "Hey, Maurine."

"How are you doing?"

"I'm fine. I owned a security company for thirty years. Remember?"

"Yes, I remember. Bet you never came up against anything like this in those thirty years, though, did you?"

"No. This is a new one. The reality of that discussion the three of us had is beginning to come into focus. Suddenly, I find myself shoulder deep in it, instead of just hearing about it."

"Yes. It would seem that way. I'm sorry."

"I don't know why. It isn't your fault."

"Please be careful out there. I would hate for anything to happen to any of you. Let's just hope you find Henry."

"Alright. I'm going to get off of the radio now. They might need it for other traffic."

"Robert's Grove, out," Maurine said.

"They aren't going to find Henry," Angie said. If they do,

it will just be pieces of him." Angie stood, looking out across the Blue Hole at the deceptively calm surface.

While Angie peered at the crystalline water of the blue hole, someone watched her from a hundred yards away. Someone with almond-shaped eyes, and elliptical pupils. Satisfied, that person, or creature, turned her back in seeming boredom and dived beneath the surface, swimming slowly away.

CHAPTER FIVE

The Search for Henry

The first search team to arrive was a Belize Coast Guard helicopter. It was equipped with pontoons, so it came in for a landing very close to the *Belize What You Want*. Divers in wet suits hopped out of the chopper carrying paddles, which they used to paddle the chopper close enough to the 'crime boat' as it would be called. A line was tossed to Oscar, who pulled their pontoon close enough to the boat so that a uniformed, official looking Belizean could step out of the chopper, onto the pontoon, and then on to the boat.

"I am Captain Crown," the uniformed man said, in a Belizean accent, without extending his hand in greeting. "Tell me what happened here." His accent was thick.

Oscar repeated his story to the captain, who listened intently. When Oscar finished, the Belizean Captain said, "Was there some kind of confronta-shan?"

Oscar looked confused. "Confrontation? No. I told you. He is my deckhand. There was no kind of confrontation at all. He was supposed to be waiting for us when we surfaced."

"You sure you didn't kill him and shove the body overboard?" the captain said, with an insolent expression on his face.

"Oh my God," Oscar said in disgust. "They sent Colombo to investigate this! Listen to me," he said to the captain, exasperated, "Nobody here did anything to Henry. If that's the best you can do, they need to send you back to your play pen and give us a real investigator. We've got a serious problem here, and we need to all be working together to find Henry. Quit fucking around, trying to be some big shot that *breaks the case*."

"Who you think you talking to?" the narcissistic captain said, offended that someone would challenge him.

"I know exactly who I'm talking to," Oscar said, his voice raised in anger. "And I know *WHAT* I am talking to! I'm talking to a demented idiot with an ego problem. A fucking narcissist with an IQ that matches his age! There! Is that clear enough for you? Listen, you might think you're going to intimidate me. But the fact is, I will report your ass and file a complaint against you if you keep on with this bullshit! Come on, try me!"

The Belizean captain, now furious that his bluff had not worked, turned and stepped over the gunwale of the boat, trying for the pontoon of the helicopter. But his foot missed the pontoon, and he fell headlong into the water with a splash. He surfaced, sputtering and cursing. The two divers, who had been waiting for instructions while standing on the pontoons, broke out in uncontrolled laughter, pointing at their captain in the water. One of them even gave Oscar a thumbs up sign, but nobody seemed in a hurry to help Captain Crown get out of the water.

The captain clambered out of the water, onto the pontoon, opened the door of the chopper and climbed in, dripping. He yelled at the pilot, "Git de fock out from here!"

The pilot started the motor of the chopper while the two divers climbed aboard, still laughing. For that matter, the pilot was laughing, too. The rotors began turning and the chopper lifted off, creating a hurricane of wind as it rose into the air.

Ten minutes later, a Sea Rescue vessel approached slowly, working its way through the coral heads. Three uniformed men stood on the bow, eyeing the *Belize What You Want.*

"Well, here we go again!" Oscar said, obviously frustrated.

But when the Sea Rescue boat approached, it slowed and one of the men on the bow of the boat waved in greeting. This was a good sign. Oscar returned the greeting. The boat dew near and one of the men tossed a line to Oscar. He quickly secured it to a chock on the gunwale.

"Permission to come aboard," one of the men said.

"Permission granted," Oscar said, and extended a hand in case the Sea Rescue officer needed steadying when crossing over.

When he was aboard, he smiled respectfully. "My name is Chad Armstrong." He shook hands with everybody. "I understand we have a problem to deal with. But first, I want to thank you." He smiled at Oscar.

"For what?" Oscar asked, curious.

"You wouldn't believe the chatter on the radio. The helicopter pilot is telling the story everywhere about your brief meeting with Captain Crown. I've never heard so much laughter. Captain Crown is, uh..."

"A brain-dead asshole? Is that the term your looking for?" Angie offered.

"I was thinking of very similar words, yes, thank you!" Chad said as he laughed. "So, he fell in the drink, eh?"

"Head-first!" Oscar said with a smile.

Chad couldn't contain himself. He laughed hard, and the two men on the bow of the boat laughed with him. It was obvious Captain Crown was something of a bad joke, even among his peers. Chad got a grip and returned to a more sober demeanor. "I apologize. Okay, to the business at hand. What happened here?"

Oscar retold the story of Henry's disappearance. When he finished, Chad looked around. "I need to call in another helicopter and do an aerial search!" Chad pulled a walkie talkie from a holder on his belt and called in aerial reinforcements. He then asked to see the blood spots. He hadn't gone very far into his investigation when he stopped and addressed Oscar, Angie, and Richard.

"I don't want you to think I'm an escapee from an asylum, but we've had some bizarre things happen around here in the past year or so. Last year, a boat load of divers just disappeared. They recovered a few of them. Then, some scuba divers, well, 'hunters' speared this really ghastly, *huge* sea creature. The place is getting a reputation like The Bermuda Triangle. Now this! I don't know if we'll find your deckhand or not. But I strongly recommend avoiding the place. We'll be glad to escort you out of here when you're ready to leave. In fact, I will insist on it. First, I have to get statements from all of you. Would you mind accompanying me onto our boat? I have the paperwork there."

While the foursome were in the large office of the Sea Rescue yacht, completing paperwork, a helicopter could be heard flying over-head. Chad's walkie talkie crackled to life.

"Air Sea Rescue Number Three, on location, Sir. We will commence our grid."

Chad took his walkie talkie in hand. "Ten-four, Air Three."

It took less than thirty minutes for Air Three to report back. "We've got something here close to the edge of the reef."

All four people rushed out of the yacht's office to stand on the deck and look to where the helicopter was. Like the first helicopter on the scene, it was equipped with pontoons. When they spotted whatever it was, the chopper slowly descended to a place less than a mile south of their location.

By using binoculars, everybody on the sea rescue yacht could see men getting out of the chopper. Then a body bag was passed down to them. A couple of minutes later, the bag was handed back to the people inside the chopper. Something human sized was in the bag. The men on the ground climbed back in the chopper and it lifted off.

The chopper flew slowly toward them. A voice came over the walkie talkie. "Somebody in that group can make a positive I-D?"

"Yeah," Chad said, "If he's the one missing from here."

"Okay, we'll land. But I think I should warn you; this victim is pretty messed up."

"Like how?" Chad asked.

There was a pause. Then, "Something tore him apart. Everything inside him is either missing entirely, or in shreds."

"Acknowledged," Chad said. Then he turned to Oscar. "I'm sorry, but we need for you to identify the victim. Can you handle it?"

Oscar nodded. "This won't be easy. But I know it's got to be done." Then he turned to Angie and Richard. "I think it would be best if you waited here, or on our boat. This doesn't sound like it's going to be fun."

"No problem," Angie said.

The chopper slowly descended to a spot only a few yards from the Sea Rescue yacht. Helpers jumped out once the blades had stopped turning and paddled the chopper up against the side of the yacht. Chad and Oscar hopped onto the pontoon of the chopper and made their way to the bay door, then climbed aboard the aircraft.

It didn't take long for Oscar to re-emerge. Once on the outside of the air/sea aircraft, he bent over and puked into the water. He was obviously very shaken, and unsteady. He grabbed hold of the bay door frame to steady himself. A minute later, he bent over and purged again. Looking pale, he made his way to the front of the pontoon and started to climb on board the Sea Rescue yacht. Then, thinking better of it, he dove into the water and swam to the dive platform on the back of *Belize What You Want*. He climbed the ladder and boarded his own boat, then sat in a lounge chair located on the stern.

Angie and Richard looked at Chad, who had managed

to reboard his own boat. "Are we through here?" Angie asked.

"I think so," Chad said. "I don't know what else we can do. Let us escort you out of here, and, for that matter, all the way back to the coast."

"I'm sure we would appreciate that," Angie said. "It's obvious there is something very intent on killing people here."

When they re-boarded the *Belize What You Want*, Oscar managed to confirm their worst fears. "Yes. It was Henry, or what's left of him. I've never seen anything that horrible in my life. He was... 'eaten'! Something just tore into him. His stomach area was... I could see his spine by looking into the hole in his stomach! His eyes were wide open. He was frightened and in pain when he died. I hope I never see anything like that again!"

———

Thirty minutes later, as the *Belize What You Want* followed the Sea Rescue yacht slowly through Lighthouse Reef, away from The Great Blue Hole and toward the small cut in the reef used to enter and exit, Angie looked back at where they had come from, as Richard stood beside her.

"Every horrible thing I felt would happen is happening," Angie said. "It's going to get worse. Something tells me it's gonna get a lot worse than ever before." If she would have been looking through her binoculars, she could have spotted that same female figure with the almond-shaped eyes and elliptical pupils watch the Belize What You Want, retreat.

CHAPTER SIX

The Warning

The sky to the north started turning dark blue. Although it was miles away, lightning could be seen playing in the clouds. "Look at that," Angie said. "Storm coming and it's not even the rainy season. It's like some kind of omen!"

Richard looked at the approaching storm but said nothing. The ship-to-shore radio came to life with Maurine's voice. "Robert's Grove Resort calling the *Belize What You Want!*

Richard was standing closest to the radio, and Oscar was sort of zoned out, in a semitrance, just following along behind the Sea Rescue vessel. So Richard answered the radio. "Hey, Maurine; what's up?"

"The chatter I'm picking up on the radio doesn't sound very good."

"I don't know what they're saying, but it would be hard to exaggerate."

"Henry?"

"No longer with us."

"Heaven help us! He has a young wife and a two-year-old daughter."

"Has anyone told her?"

"I don't know. I'll go to their house as soon as we end this call."

Richard shook his head. "Such a tragedy. And we don't even know what happened."

"What do you think happened?"

"No, no. Not over the radio. Angie and I will fill you in when we get there."

"Well, how's Oscar?"

"Devastated. Can't talk more about it here. We're about an hour out. We'll see you there."

"Okay, I'll be waiting."

Richard hung up the microphone. "Man, that's tough," he said, as he shook his head. "Young mother with a baby to raise. Young father killed by...who knows what!"

"A bleeding goddamned mother-fucking bitch from hell!" Oscar started screaming, even though he was steering the boat. "Let's quit pussyfooting around! We all know what happened!"

Richard was shocked. "Well, not all of us. Enlighten me."

"It's the sister! The sister of Maris, the siren. She's pissed off because this one," he pointed at Angie, "killed her sister, or was responsible for it."

"It had to be done!" Angie screamed back.

"Yas, I know, I know. Yas, it had to be done. But I just don't want to tiptoe around what we're dealing with here. Let's at least tell the fucking *truth*! And the fucking truth is, we've got monsters straight out of mythology books right here in goddamned Belize. And those monsters are killing people!

"Actually, I guess I'm grateful that you killed the one sister. But now, *finish the job*. Don't leave us with an insane, wild, enraged sister from hell that none of us knows how to deal with. She'll wind up killing us all! Belize will wind up a pile of bleached bones. It'll look like Jonestown around here."

"Oscar," Angie said. "Why do you think I'm down here? That's what I'm here to do."

Oscar looked Angie straight in the eye. "If you mean that, I'll give you any kind of help that you ask for. A lot of other people will too. Just please don't stop until this nightmare is brought to an end."

Angie returned Oscar's gaze. "You have my word," she said very solemnly.

The sky was growing darker. The storm was closing in. Now, the rumble of thunder could be heard faintly in the distance. More lightning could be seen playing in the clouds.

An hour later, both vessels pulled up to the pier at Robert's Grove Resort. People saw them coming and ran out on the pier to catch the tie-off lines when they were thrown. It was starting to rain, so the boats were quickly secured, and people started disembarking. Angie and Richard grabbed their diving equipment and ran toward the main cluster of buildings, and their rooms.

Maurine met them in front of the office door, beneath the overhang. Angie paused just long enough to tell Maurine, "I'm going to go take a shower. I'll see you in the bar. I need about a dozen of those Siren's Potions." Then she ran on by. But as she left, Maurine hollered to her, "Look in the closet. There's an umbrella there."

Richard stopped to talk to Maurine for a moment, and Chad joined them.

"Did you talk to Henry's wife?" Richard asked Maurine.

"Yes, I did. The doctor is with her now. She didn't take it well."

"I can only imagine," Richard said.

Chad said he needed to leave. Now that the *Belize What You Want* was safely in port, his job was done. He tipped his hat, said his goodbyes, and retreated through the rain to his yacht. He passed Oscar en route and stopped for a quick moment to say something to him. Oscar shook his head yes, shook hands with Chad, then hurried toward Maurine and Richard.

Oscar stopped where Maurine and Richard were standing, just long enough to be polite, but then left to go to his house. As he walked away, Maurine said, "I've already been to Henry's house and spoken with his wife."

"I appreciate that," Oscar said. "I wasn't looking forward to telling her."

"I was afraid something like this might happen," Maurine said to Richard as both of them stood close to keep out of the rain, which was growing heavier.

"What do you mean?" Richard asked.

"Angie is a very special woman. Unique, actually. She has a sixth sense unlike anybody I have ever known. She came down here because she had a premonition. Every time she has had a premonition in the past, she has been amazingly accurate. I've never seen anything like it. She just had to go out to the Blue Hole to look for that 'something' that she felt. If I had any sense, I should have sent the entire Belize Coast Guard with her. Once again, she was right. And now, we have another dead body, another tragedy, another broken family. I feel responsible because I didn't follow my own instinct and do what I felt needed to be done to protect all of you today."

"I don't know what practical thing you could have done. Angie is also a pretty independent woman. She would have probably 'pshawed' any suggestion you made regarding security."

"Maybe. Maybe not. But I know one thing. In the future, I will keep my ear to the ground a lot better, and when Angie goes off on another tangent of any kind, I'll have the cavalry surround her so that she doesn't wind up with an obituary."

"Probably a good idea," Richard said, then split off from Maurine so that he could go to his room and clean up.

———

Later that evening, in the restaurant, Angie slouched in her chair, while outside, thunder rolled. The smell of the rain was sweet and made a comfortable atmosphere. But it was an aura that Angie didn't seem to notice. She was half in the bag. Richard sat across from her, leaning back in his chair, hands folded, seeming a little bit at a loss. Maurine approached the table and sat down. She had a cup of hot tea in her hand.

"The rain is kind of nice," Maurine said. She didn't get a response from either of her guests. "You need something to eat," she said. It wasn't a question, but rather a statement.

Maurine then said, hoping for a response, "Seafood? A fruit salad? A sixty ounce T bone?

"Maybe just as soon as my stomach quits doing flip flops," Angie answered, never noticing Maurine's attempt at a quip.

Switching subjects, Maurine asked, "Do you think it's Maris, reincarnated from the whatever?"

After a few seconds, "No," Angie replied. "I know for an absolute certainty that it is not Maris."

"Oh! How?"

Angie looked straight at her glass, then took a deep sip of her Siren's Potion. "Because Maris's idea of a good time, that is to say, her favorite form of mayhem was to morph into a grotesque monster with a huge maw, open that maw and take her victim's entire head into her mouth... her 'maw', and bite down until she heard the skull pop, then bite her victim's face off. By the time she got through, there wasn't much left of her victim's head. But more importantly, that's how she did it *every time, without fail, no exceptions!*"

"So?"

"Henry was disemboweled. His head was never touched. Different modus operandi. Creatures hunt according to patterns. Maris wasn't human. She was a creature, a deadly creature who was two thousand years old, but a creature, nonetheless. Besides, I saw Maris turn into a Post Toasty, right in front of my eyes. So, it wasn't Maris. Maris is dead. Permanently dead.

"Now, we're probably dealing with her sister. At least that's what Oscar believes, and I concur. There was a sister mentioned in that book out at the ranch, but she didn't receive much press. The writer didn't think she posed much of a threat. But now, something has a burr under her saddle, and she's come full bloom. She is no longer content to remain upstage, in the background, benign. She's here to cause as much shit and destruction as she can."

"Meaning she's going on a killing spree?" Richard offered.

"Yep. Exactly that. She's every bit as crazy as her sister, and now she's out for revenge. Problem is, I don't know what I'm dealing with this time. I don't know what she looks like, whether or not she can morph. I'm assuming that she can."

"So, what are you saying?"

"I'm saying that I don't know what I'm doing. I don't know whether to shit or go blind, and I hope I don't fuck this up. If I do, people are going to die. I need a plan, and I don't have one. At this point, the only thing I've got…"

"We," Richard interrupted.

"What?"

"We! If you think I'm going to sit here and let you take this thing on alone, all by your lonesome, you've got monkeys with yoyos playing in your head. You need an assistant, a side-kick. One that has training in dealing with 'mayhem.' So… 'we'."

Angie almost smiled as she looked at Richard. "Alright, 'we.' The only thing *we* have is absolute confirmation that something is out there, and 'it' is dangerous. Maybe… no, 'probably' more dangerous than Maris ever thought of being. Maris killed because she was frightened for her existence. There wasn't anger involved, so much as fear. Paranoia. She felt like discovery translated to extinction, and in a way, she was right. She was just trying to protect her territory. This new 'thing' is furious. No, enraged! It wants to kill to get even."

Maurine looked at Richard. She tried to hide the concern in her eyes. "Are you sure you know what you're getting into?" She asked him.

"No," Richard confessed. "But I do know that I am not going to let this brave young woman go walking into this uncertain valley alone. She needs somebody at her side."

"I appreciate that 'young' comment! Thank you, Richard. No matter how inaccurate it might be," Angie said.

"You're a good man, Richard Hart. Maybe the best I have ever met," Maurine said, looking straight at Richard with an expression of admiration on her face.

Well, maybe. Maybe it wasn't that simple. *Maybe* Dr. Maurine Howard was falling in love with this man who didn't seem to know the meaning of the word, 'fear', and was so giving of himself. And maybe Maurine knew she was falling in love, maybe she didn't.

"If a man has something to give, and doesn't give it, then he cheats himself as well as everyone around him," Richard was saying with a smile.

"That's beautiful," Maurine said.

"It happens to be the truth," Richard said.

"Let's hear it for truth," Angie said, raising her glass.

The three friends clinked glasses and a cup, then drank. Richard's mood turned slightly somber. "Truth! It's a strange thing. It keeps changing, like colors on a movie screen."

"What are you talking about?" Angie asked.

"At the moment, I'm talking about who I am, opposed to who I used to be. What you see before you is basically the 'new' Richard. There was a time in my life when I wasn't such a nice guy. Actually, I was a twenty-four-karat sonofabitch; a gun toting hood who just happened to be on the right side of the law. Then, one day, I had an epiphany. I woke up and realized what a lucky mother f...well, just how lucky I was. I couldn't even begin to count my blessings, starting with the fact that, for some reason, God had given me a wonderful, loving woman. And I had been neglecting her. There were times I did worse than that.

"How?" Maurine asked.

"Well, there's that word 'truth,' again. I wasn't true to her. One day, I looked in the mirror, and I didn't like who I saw. Didn't like him at all. So, I turned my life around. Began a new chapter, a new philosophy, a new code of rules to live by. Now, I like me a lot better. The last few years with Angela were good ones. I gave her the respect and love she deserved. Even to the point that I fawned over her. Then, for some reason, God took her away from me."

"Do you mind if I ask what happened to her?"

"Heart gave out. I think it was all those years that I wasn't home. I was out drinking, whoring. She sat home. She knew what I was doing. I think it affected her heart. I will take that to my grave. There is no way to forgive myself." Tears came to Richard's eyes. "That's the reason that now, I'm very careful that what I do doesn't hurt somebody else. I never want to cause pain again for as long as I live. I just hope there is a heaven." Then he stopped. He was too choked up to talk.

Maurine's expression was one of empathy. Very softly, she said, "My God! A man with a conscience! How rare is that? More importantly, where has he been all of my life?"

Just then, there was a horrendous explosion somewhere outside. The shockwave was felt strongly in the restaurant and knocked glasses off of the shelf. Everybody in the restaurant jumped in surprise, then dashed outside to see what had happened.

There was nothing left of the *Belize What You Want* except for a little bit of the hull floating close to the dock, and that was on fire. Also, the pier close to where Oscar had tied the boat up was shattered.

"What the hell is that?" Richard said. "Some kind of warning?"

"I seriously doubt it," Angie said. "An ancient creature of the sea, using explosives? Not likely. It might be a warning, but it wasn't from her."

"Who then?" Maurine asked.

"I don't know," Angie said, as she turned to go back to her table. "This fucking thing just keeps getting better and better. But somebody's got a hard on, you can believe that."

Oscar showed up, stopped adjacent to everybody watching the fire, and said, "Was that my boat?"

"So, it appears," Angie said.

"What the hell happened?"

"Well, it seems that it blew the fuck up," Angie said. "I'm thinking that I'm glad it didn't happen while we were on board. Is there somebody that's pissed off at you?" Angie asked Oscar.

Oscar turned from looking at the flames in the water to Angie. "What? No. Not that I can think of."

"Think harder. That boat didn't blow itself up."

The local police arrived in the Robert's Grove parking lot. Uniformed cops started bailing out of the car, opening umbrellas, looking remarkably similar to *The Keystone Cops*, and came running through the rain, to the people gathered in front of the restaurant.

"What happened here?" one of them asked, in his thick Belizean accent.

"Why don't you take a wild guess," Angie said.

The cop looked at her for a moment, then back at the fire. Some of the other cops were trying to make their way out onto the wrecked pier while holding their umbrellas. Their reason for doing so was unclear. One of them went a little too far out. The weakened pier gave way beneath him and sent him plummeting into the water, shouting an oath as the water splashed. Two of his compadres helped him out of the water, while another one turned around and came back to where the one cop was standing, who was apparently in charge. "We need to put out that fire," the cop said.

"What for?" Angie said. "There is just only so far that hull can burn down in the water. Besides, have you noticed? It's raining! The rain will put it out."

"What if it drifts and sets some other boats on fire?"

"Does it look like it's drifting?" Angie asked, with a hint of insolence in her voice. "Well," she continued. "The fuzz are here, so I guess we're all safe. Fuck it, let's go back inside and continue what we were doing... mainly, drinking!"

Motioning toward the dock, Maurine said, "But there was an explosion out there on my dock."

"Yeah," Angie said. "That's kind of what it looks like. You coming? I mean, it's dark out here, except for light from the fire. Whatcha going to do? Can't do much until in the morning, when there's daylight to see by and the rain has stopped. You need to investigate, assess the damage and the needed repairs. Schedule workers, yada yada yada! But you can't do any of that right now, so chill! Come help me get drunk so we can figure this thing out. There's 'something' going on, and we need to break the code before we can formulate a plan to deal with it."

"I hate to say this," Richard said, "but she's actually kind of right."

"Well, alright," Maurine said, looking up at the dark sky. "Let me talk to one of my men over here, and I'll be in there in a minute."

CHAPTER SEVEN

Aria Revealed

Richard followed Angie back to the table and took a seat. After emptying her glass and finding the waiter, who was just coming back into the restaurant from outside, where he had been watching the fire, she motioned to him for another drink. Then Angie turned her attention to Richard.

"I feel that I need to make it crystal clear that 'something' around here wants to kill me. Oscar is right. It is most likely Maris's sister. And if you help me, she is going to get the red-ass at you and try to kill you, too."

"Angie, I don't really care too much whether I live or die. I just want to make redress for my sins before I take the big hickey."

"Redress! Well, okay. I guess we all have to face our own demons."

Richard smiled at Angie. "Don't you have any demons, Angie?"

"Yeah, I guess. We all have demons," Angie admitted. But she wasn't about to get specific. "What I want to focus on right now is the demon we are about to face. And she is a dangerous bitch demon!"

"Any ideas?"

"No. I'm at a loss. You know, the last time I went through this, I had some help from a couple of very unexpected people. People right out of the pages of Mythology. They aren't here this time, and my ass is really hanging in the breeze." The waiter brought her a new drink. She thanked him and took a deep sip. "The only thing we can do is wait." Then, "Wonder why those special people haven't showed up for this party?" She looked at nothing while she posed the question.

"For what?"

"What?"

"What are we waiting for?" Richard asked.

"We are waiting for her to reveal herself."

"How do you know she will?"

"Oh, she will! If she's anything like her sister, her ancient ego is going to get in her way."

"I hope she reveals herself soon," Richard said. "I'm not very good at waiting."

"Neither am I," Angie said. "Neither am I."

———

Later that night, as Angie slept comfortably in her bed, she was awakened by a female voice. "Go away from this place," the voice said, threateningly. "You are not wanted here!"

Angie tried to wake from her deep sleep. She rose up slightly in the bed. "What?" she said.

"I will not warn you again," the female voice said.

Then, in the darkness, Angie thought she made out the figure of someone walking out of the room. A moment later, she heard a sound that was reminiscent of a large bird taking flight. She didn't know if she had been dreaming, or if it was real. She got out of bed and walked to the door. It was wide open. She had been careful to lock it when she came back to her room and before she went to bed. Apparently, this had been her first contact with 'her.'

Maybe. But what was that with the sound of a bird taking flight? That made no sense. Or did it? The original three sirens were reported to be half human, half bird. Stories varied about which half was which, but that didn't matter. Could it be that the sister morphed between being a bird and a human? If so, they had their first clue. It might also help explain how Henry got from the dive boat to a point almost a mile away.

Angie doubted that 'the sister' would make a repeat appearance, but she loaded the bang stick just in case, and sat it beside her bed.

"Okay!" Angie said, sitting at a table on the deck near the restaurant the next morning. "Our enemy has made her first appearance. She is identified!"

Angie told Maurine and Richard about her brief, but startling nocturnal experience. Then she appeared tired. "I can't keep doing this. As much as I love it here at Robert's Grove, I can't keep taking on these goddamned mythological creatures, demons, whatever the fuck they are. There's got to be an end to it. Or I have to be able to pass the baton to somebody else."

She fell silent while she ate her breakfast. When she was finished, she excused herself, saying, "I didn't get much sleep last night. Now it's catching up to me. Please excuse me. I need to go to my room and sleep for a while." With that, Angie rose and walked to her room.

When she was gone, Maurine said, "Honestly, I don't know how she's lasted as long as she has. Angie has an incredible drive about her."

"It seems more like she is being driven, to me," Richard said, a concerned look on his face.

———

It was about three o'clock in the afternoon when the Robert's Grove limo pulled into the parking lot and four passengers disembarked: Scott Carrington, Al Harmon, James Harmon, and a beautiful blond woman named Chelsey Johnson.

Resort workers grabbed their luggage and brought it to the reception area. Maurine and Dolly were behind the reception desk when the group arrived. Maurine came out from behind the desk to greet the three people that she knew with a hug and shake hands with the blonde.

"Where's Angie?" Scott asked.

"I think she's in her room," Maurine answered. "She didn't get much sleep last night, so she's playing catch up."

"Which room?"

"Number four. Her favorite."

Scott departed, and Maurine turned her attention to her

other guests. Dolly also greeted them all by sniffing each person.

"It's good to see you," Maurine said. "To what do I owe this unexpected surprise?"

Al half whispered, "I needed to bring that special '*implement*' that Angie requested. James is here out of curiosity. And we just met this young woman on the plane."

"Chelsey Johnson," the woman said, extended her hand in greeting.

"Maurine Howard," Maurine said. "Here on holiday?"

"No. I'm a reporter. North Star Magazine. I've been sent down here to report on whatever it is that's going on here."

"Going on? Well, good luck with that. We have scuba diving, deep sea fishing and the jungle cruise that is very popular. Also, people like to sunbathe beside any of our three pools or hang out at the beach."

"Nice try," Chelsey said. "I'd like to meet Ms. Angie Holland.

"Okay, I imagine when she comes up here to the restaurant or bar, you can meet her."

"Can't you tell her that I'm here?"

"I'm not in the habit of disturbing guests, Ms. Johnson. Why don't you just relax until she comes into the bar. Let me offer you a drink on the house?" Maurine said, as she motioned Chelsey Johnson toward the bar, where the three men had already gone. "We have a specialty here that we call the *Siren's Potion*. I think you'll like it. It will help you 'relax'."

An hour later, Chelsey was indeed relaxed. She hadn't been prepared for the potency of the Siren's Potion. "Oh my!" she exclaimed. "What do you call this thing?" she asked the bartender.

"Siren's Potion," the bartender answered.

"How did you ever come up with that name for it?"

"I don't know, Ma'am. I don't name dem, I just make dem."

Just then, Angie, followed by Richard, Scott, Al, James and Maurine entered the bar and took seats at a rather large, round table. Chelsey saw them, slid off of her stool at the bar and walked over to their table. Looking at Angie, she said, "Excuse me. Are you Angie Holland?"

"That's the rumor," Angie answered.

"May I join you?" Chelsey asked.

"I don't know why not," Angie answered. "We're fixing to go where it looks like you already are."

"Thank you," Chelsey said. "Yes, those 'potion' things pack quite a wallop."

The bartender came to the table. "Surprise us!" Angie said. The bartender smiled and retreated behind the bar.

"I think I'd better stop drinking and get something to eat," Chelsey said. "What do you recommend?"

"The robalo mojo de ajo is the best you will find anywhere," Richard said.

"I... I'm afraid I don't know what that is!" Chelsey said.

"Snook, baked in a clay oven with garlic sauce."

"I thought snook was a pool game."

"That's Snooker. Snook is a fish. Never been to the Caribbean before, have you?" Al asked with a wry smile. And it wasn't really a question.

"Once...on a cruise."

"Why are you here?" Angie asked.

"To do a story about you. I work for the North Star magazine."

"A story about me? I can't imagine a more boring topic to write about. I don't understand. Who, specifically, sent you here, and on what premise?"

"There are a lot of rumors about you, Ms. Holland. My magazine wants to see how much truth there is to them."

"Rumors? Who would waste time spreading rumors about me? Wait! Is North Star one of those newspaper magazines you see in racks by the check-out at a grocery store?"

"That's one of our distribution points, yes."

"Oh, heaven help us! Why don't you go back to wher-ever you came from? There's no story here."

"What about that guy who disappeared yesterday, out at Lighthouse Reef?"

"Gotta ask the Coast Guard about that. It isn't my story."

"And didn't a boat blow up here last night?"

"Yep. Happens sometimes. Gas leak in the engine room. Fumes ignite when they find an ignition source. That's hardly news."

Chelsey looked down for a minute, then back up at Angie. "At the risk of pushing a point, what about all that stuff last year?"

Angie looked at Chelsey without saying anything.

"Bet I can guess where you're from," Chelsey said, changing the subject.

"Really? And what is that going to prove?" Angie said.

"It'll prove we have something in common."

"Okay," Angie said, "Guess."

"Two words," Chelsey said. "Crimson Tide. Here's three more words, KAPPA KAPPA GAMMA."

Angie's eyes got big. "Oh my God, we're sorority sisters!" She immediately rose from her chair and embraced her sorority sister from Alabama. Thus began a chat that lasted an hour. But at the end of it, Chelsey offered this; "I'll make you a deal. Let me stay and watch what you do. I give you my absolute oath that I will not write a word until it is the proper time. And when I do write a story, I will submit it to you for review and approval before I forward it to my editor. You have my promise as a sister KAPPA."

Angie thought for a minute. "I don't know how I could refuse you. Okay, but only because you gave your word. So, what years did you attend AU?"

"2000–2002. Majored in journalism. Then I wound up working for this rag. But they pay good, and a girl has to make a living!"

"Don't you feel a little bit like a whore?"

"Yeah, a little. But I'd like to think it's not permanent. Actually, I'd like to start writing books."

Angie got a thoughtful look on her face. "Speaking of whores, was a Professor Hicks still there when you attended?"

"Margaret Hicks?"

"Yeah."

"She was diabetic and had to have a leg amputated. But she was still kicking ass with the other one! Probably dead by now...pickled liver!"

"She used to keep a flask in her purse. Always stunk like a gin mill!"

The two women laughed. By now, the men had wandered off somewhere else. They were outnumbered by these gossiping females. And at some point, Maurine Howard had gotten in the middle of it, although she had gone to a different school and mostly listened in while Angie and Chelsey yakked away. Women's chatter is a formidable thing, and any male with the sense that God gave a swamp chigger stays the hell out of it. In this case, Al Harmon, James Harmon, Richard and Scott Carrington threw in the towel hours ago!

They wandered outside to the explosion site to look around. The remnants of the hull of *Belize What You Want,* had been dragged up onto the sand beach. There wasn't much left between the explosion and the fire.

"You think it was arson?" Scott asked Al.

"Impossible to say," Al said. "With everything that Angie suspects, it's a possibility. But if we're facing a sea creature here, then, like Angie, I can't see her...or him, using explosives."

"Remember Maris fooling with the electrical system on *SIREN SONG*?" Scott said.

"Yeah, that's a good point," Al said.

"The only way to find out what caused the explosion is through forensic tests," Richard said. "And I doubt these cops down here have the facilities for that."

Al Looked up at Richard. "Who the hell are you, anyway?" Al asked.

"Oh, I'm sorry," Richard said, extending his hand in greeting. "My name is Richard Johnson. I'm just an old fart that Angie met on the plane coming down here and took mercy on me."

"How much mercy?" Scott quickly asked.

Richard chuckled. "Thank you for the compliment! Actually, I was going to go out to Ambergris Caye. Then Angie recommended this place. My plans were rather disorganized, so I decided to come here instead. So far, I've learned how to scuba dive, been to The Great Blue Hole, been indirect party to a crew member disappearing, then, that crew member being found dead. It's been eventful! Something I would probably have missed on Ambergris Caye!"

"Probably!" James interjected.

Al walked over to the pier at the point where it had been shattered by the explosion. There were pieces of the boat cabin scattered around. Al stood there, looking, one arm of his sunglasses on his mouth. "You know," he said. "I am anything but an expert on explosions. But to me, it doesn't look like this explosion happened internally. It looks like it came from the top of the boat!"

"Impossible!" Richard said.

"You would think so," Al said. "But look at those pieces of the cabin top. The fiberglass is shattered, but the metal braces are bent down, like something on top of the boat exploded!"

"But what?" Scott asked.

"Lightning," Al said.

"He's right," Richard said. "The explosion didn't come from the engine room or inside the cabin. It couldn't have! So, lightning makes sense."

The four men dug deeper into their investigation. Meanwhile, the three women, with Dolly the dog, made their way out onto the deck close to a swimming pool. By now, they were having their own party. Be that as it may, Angie cleverly kept one eye open for any new woman that might be watching them closer than usual.

Maurine's phone rang. She picked it up from the table, said "Robert's Grove Resort," and listened for a minute. Then, "Anybody we know?"

When she said this, the other two women fell silent and tried to listen to Maurine's phone call. Finally, Maurine said, "Thank you," and ended the call. She looked squarely at Angie and said, "You're off the hook."

"I didn't realize I was on the hook. What do you mean?"

"There's been another mysterious death at the Blue Hole. Same scenario. Woman disappeared from the stern of a yacht while other people on the boat were diving. They found her about a half mile away, among the coral heads, with her midsection missing, completely eaten. Torn open and eaten. Whoever this, *whatever* this is, it's more dangerous than Maris ever thought of being."

Chelsey looked at Angie. "I thought you told me there wasn't a story here, Sister!"

"That may have changed," Angie said. "Or gotten bigger."

Angie rose from her seat to walk out on the pier and tell the men.

CHAPTER EIGHT

Plane Crash in the Jungle

The next day found the group, including Angie, Chelsey Johnson Scott, and Richard Hart in a small airplane, flying over the Blue Hole. Richard hired the plane and pilot, named Niles, thinking it might be of some benefit to take a good look at everything from the air.

Angie was quietly desperate for some clue, a thread, something to work with in order to formulate a plan. At this point, she wasn't even sure what she was dealing with. All she knew was it was dangerous, and it wanted to kill. Apparently, it didn't matter who, just so long as it killed somebody! Well, that might have changed now that Angie was here because apparently, it knew who she was, and knew why she was here. It was better informed than she was. But how?

Niles circled the Blue Hole several times, starting at about fifteen hundred feet, then dropped down a little with each revolution until he was only a few hundred feet above the water. A Belize Coast Guard boat was on station at the Blue Hole, to make sure no pleasure crafts came in for any tourist activity. There was also another Coast Guard boat on station near the narrow opening in Lighthouse Reef, which led to the hole.

Angie was somber as she looked out the window of the plane, down at the hole. Richard had brought along a camera and stayed busy snapping pictures. Chelsey was the only one in the group that seemed enthralled, looking out the window, making frequent comments as the plane circled.

"It looks like something from another planet," Chelsey said, wide eyed. "And you have all been diving there?"

"Yes," came the collective answer.

But nothing out of the ordinary was seen by the searchers, so Richard asked Niles to return to Placencia. The pilot turned the plane toward shore and climbed up to about five thousand feet. Everything was droning along uneventfully for a few minutes. Then something hit against the plane's fuselage, hard. It was somewhere behind where the passenger seats were located. Almost everyone on the plane screamed, even the men, except for Niles, the pilot, who was too busy trying to get control of the aircraft.

"I'm having trouble keeping control of her," he said as he wrestled with the helm.

"What do you mean?" Richard asked, who was sitting in the co-pilot's seat.

"We're slowly losing altitude, and she's veering to port. I can't bring her back on course." Niles turned on his microphone. "Mayday, Mayday! This is Tropic Airlines R211. I'm east of Placencia, forty miles out. But the aircraft is pointed south of there, and I have little control. Mayday, Mayday!"

Niles listened for a response. There was none. "Whatever hit us must have damaged the antenna," he said.

"What's he saying?" Angie asked from the seat behind Richard.

"He's calling for help," Richard said, loud enough for Angie to hear.

"Why? Are we going down?" she yelled.

"Don't know." Then Richard yelled at Niles, "Are we going to make it?"

"Not if I can't correct this course," Niles said. "We'll wind up in the jungle, south of Placencia. Probably won't even be in Belize anymore. Maybe Guatemala! We're slowly losing altitude and I can't seem to pull her up!"

"Oh, shit!" Richard said.

"What?" Angie asked.

Richard hollered over his shoulder. "Get on your cell phone and call Maurine. Tell her we're going down."

"Sonofabitch!" Angie said and dug her cell phone out of her belt holder. She tried to dial Maurine's number, but there was no signal this far out. "No signal," she yelled. "I'll keep trying until I get a bar."

Meanwhile, the small, six-seater plane continued to slowly descend and slowly veer to the south. By the time they reached the mainland, they were barely a thousand feet above the jungle canopy. The plane was trying to list to port, and Niles was having a hell of a time trying to keep it level.

"I want everyone to brace for impact," Niles yelled. "We're going to have to ditch in this damned jungle. I just hope I can find a clearing!"

Ten minutes later. They were still airborne, but barely

above the treetops. Niles spotted what he thought might be a bald spot a couple of miles ahead, and slightly to port. "I'm gonna have to try for there!" he said, clearly worried.

By the time the plane approached the bald spot, the plane was clipping treetops. And the bald spot was bald, it turned out, because Indians had chosen this spot for a slash and burn milpa (corn field). They had cut down the trees and burned most of the hardwood, but there were still stumps remaining, protruding from the ground by as much as three feet.

"Oh, shit!" Niles said, when he saw the stumps. But he had no choice at this point. He was committed. The plane was going down. All Niles could do was try to aim the aircraft so that it hit as few of the stumps as possible. He put the props in reverse in an attempt to slow the craft as much as possible, and revved the engines, but there just wasn't enough time. Within seconds, the plane fell the last few feet to the ground and began sliding through the debris left over from the slash and burn efforts. It only took seconds for both wings to be ripped off as the plane skidded through tree stumps, some as big around as fifty-five-gallon drums.

There was a horrible screeching of metal against wood and rock, and loud booming sounds when the fuselage bounced from hitting objects on the jungle floor. The fuselage hit one stump almost head on, causing the nose to rise in the air, then slam back down to the ground with a sickening thump.

What was left of the aircraft reached the edge of the clearing, and kept going into thick underbrush, finally slowing and coming to a stop in dense growth beside a sapodilla tree. The fact that anyone survived was a miracle.

The windshield was shattered, and the passenger side bay door torn off.

Richard was barely conscious and bleeding from a deep scratch on his left shoulder. His head was swimming, but he managed to gain composure enough to begin checking on everyone else. He looked to his left. Niles had his head laid back, his eyes wide open, and a piece of wood protruding through the left side of his neck, which had apparently hit the carotid artery. Richard felt for a pulse and confirmed that Niles had none. He was dead.

Richard managed to wrestle the door beside him open and crawl out, so that he could go to the missing passenger door and check on the other three people in the plane. They were all a little bloody and Scott was unconscious, but all three were alive. Richard managed to unsnap their safety belts and drag them, one by one, out of the plane. He observed that at least no smoke was curling up from what was left of the airplane. With the wings and engines gone, at least there would be no fuel to ignite a fire.

Angie was the first one to start coming around. She moved her head from side to side, muttering, "Turn the thermostat down, Scott!"

Richard pulled her hair back out of her face. "Angie! Can you hear me? It's Richard!"

There was a pause. Then, "Richard? What are you doing in my bed?"

"Open your eyes, Angie!" Richard said. "You aren't in bed. You've been in a plane crash."

Angie wrinkled her brow, but then did manage to open her eyes and looked around, wall eyed for a moment. "Plane crash? Am I dead?"

"No. Thank providence for that. Wake up! You've got to help me revive Scott and Chelsey."

"Scott? Who's Chelsey? Oh, wait. I remember. Is Scott alright?" Angie was forcing herself to come to the surface. She had incredible will power.

"Check and make sure you can move your head and arms alright, then your legs. Any sharp pains anywhere?" Richard asked.

Angie followed Richard's instructions. "I'm dizzy," Angie reported. "But I think I'm alright." As soon as her head quit spinning enough, she turned to Scott, who was lying on the ground to her left, and started trying to revive him.

Meanwhile, Richard went to Chelsey, who was moaning, but seemed alright, and was waking up on her own. "What happened?" she asked.

"You were in a plane crash, Chelsey," Richard answered.

"My knee hurts," Chelsey said. Richard looked down at Chelsey's knee. She was wearing some kind of loose summer shorts, so her knee wasn't covered by anything. The knee looked red and bruised but didn't appear to be broken.

"I'll help you up in a minute, and let's see if you can walk on it," Richard said.

Chelsey was coming around. "Walk? Walk where?"

"To safety, for starters," Richard said. "Come on, snap out of it, Chelsey. We're in a spot here, and we all need to be thinking straight and pulling together."

"Well, I wanted a story! Looks like I got one," Chelsey said, as she stood up and tried to pull herself together, brushing her hair back with her hand, and visually checking different parts of herself.

"Did your camera survive?" she asked Richard.

"I have no idea. Right now, I'm worried about us surviving."

"Of course. Mind if I look for it?" Chelsey asked.

"Sure, go ahead," Richard said. By now, he was trying to help Angie attend to Scott. Chelsey walked over to the plane, or what was left of it, and started looking around in the passenger side. Then she looked up and saw Niles, his head laid back against the seat, his eyes open, staring blankly at nothing. Chelsey was stunned. Her eyes grew large, and her mouth fell open. She backed away from the plane. Then pointed toward it. "The...the...the pilot...is..."

"Dead. Yes, I know," Richard finished Chelsey's sentence for her.

"He's got something... a piece of wood, I think..."

"Sticking into his throat," Richard finished. "Chelsey, that is a tragedy. But we have one person dead, and four that are still alive. That is more than a minor miracle. Which ones do you imagine require the most attention right now?"

"Of course," Chelsey said, as she seemed to snap out of it and face the situation at hand. "Tell me what to do," she added.

Scott began to come around. "What the fuck happened?" he asked.

"Plane crash," Angie said, as she raised Scott up and rested him on her lap. "Oh... yeah. Now I remember," Scott said. "Damn! It's a miracle that we're still alive! Did I shit my pants? Because when we hit those first trees..."

"I don't know," Angie said. "And I'm not going to check to find out."

"Is everybody alright?" Scott asked. "Everybody survive?"

"Not the pilot. He isn't with us anymore."

"Niles? Aw man! He's a nice guy."

"Was, Scott. Yes, he was. His excellent flying is the only reason any of us survived."

"What the hell was it that hit the plane?"

"I don't know specifically what it was," Angie said, anger now in her voice. "But I'll bet I know who is responsible for it."

"Maris's sister!"

"None other. If we needed any other confirmation that she exists, we have it now as far as I am concerned."

Chelsey had worked her way around to the opposite side of Scott from where Angie was, so she could be in a position to help if needed. Richard happened to glance at the tree behind Chelsey.

"Everybody freeze, right now!" Richard said.

Everybody took Richard at his word and froze. Richard looked around and spotted a tree branch about eight feet long and half as big around as a baseball bat. It had been snapped off of some nearby tree when the plane came skidding in. Richard seized it and walked toward Chelsey, but slightly to her right.

"I want you to walk slowly, straight ahead, Chelsey. Even if it means stepping over Scott," Richard said, but not looking at Chelsey when he said it. Chelsey instantly obeyed. As soon as she moved forward, Richard stepped to where she had been standing and carefully placed the stick on top of the head of a seven-foot-long fer-de-lance. Before the snake had a chance to react, Richard reached down and seized it behind the head. He dropped the stick and used his other hand to grab the snake around the body. "I'll be right back," Richard said.

Once again, Chelsey was open mouthed with awe. "That thing could have killed me!" she uttered.

"Most likely," Angie concurred.

Richard reemerged a couple of minutes later, without the snake.

"Did you kill it?" Chelsey asked.

"No," Richard replied. "I took it a couple of hundred feet away from us and turned it loose."

"Whaaaat?" Chelsey said. "Why didn't you kill it?"

"Because it lives here," Richard said matter of factly.

"But it might come back!"

"Not likely," Richard said, reassuringly. "That snake doesn't want any more to do with us than we do with it."

"You're a righteous dude!" Scott said. Scott was feeling better, albeit still a little woozy, but close to making an attempt at standing, especially after seeing the snake so close by.

"You think you're okay?" Angie asked.

"As long as I have your love, I'll always be okay," Scott said, with an attempt at a smile.

"Alright! He's not hurt too bad!" Angie said, and stood up, then helped Scott get on his feet.

"Alright," Angie said. "What do we do next?"

"We start walking out of here," Richard said.

"Wait a minute! I thought the rule of thumb was to remain with an aircraft in a situation like this," Chelsey said.

"You saw that fer-de-lance," Richard said, looking at her.

"You want to stick around until dark, when some of his buddies show up and you can't see them coming? You can do that. We're leaving."

Chelsey looked shocked. "No. I hate snakes. Any kind of snake."

"Then you'll really hate that one. If he bites you, you'll be dead in a few minutes. We need to start walking out in the direction the plane flew in. We know the coast is over there somewhere. So, look at the sun and set your mental compass by it."

"What about Niles?" Chelsey asked.

"What about him?" Angie answered. "There's nothing we can do for him. Look, Chelsey, there's a time, and a place to be a bleeding heart. This is not the time, or the place. We've got to focus on saving our own asses. Again, there's nothing we can do for Niles. Unfortunate, for sure! But true. When this is over, there'll be people here to investigate the crash. They'll bag him up and do the right thing, take his body to a funeral home, whatever. That is not our job. Our job is to survive, and we can't do that standing around here with our finger up our ass. Now, let's go! Richard, please take point. We'll follow you."

"Let's go," Richard said, and began walking in the direction the plane had flown in from. Chelsey fell in behind Richard, followed by Angie, and then Scott followed up the rear. They only went a couple of hundred yards before they came to the cleared spot in the jungle.

"Seems like if Indians cleared this area to plant corn, they wouldn't be too far from here," Richard said. "Maybe they saw the plane come down."

"You think?"

"Hard to say."

"Okay, so what kind of Indians are we talking about?" Scott asked.

"I don't know all that much about Belize," Richard answered. "You've been down here several times, from what I've been told. Don't you know?"

Nah. We've been here, but always on dive trips. Still, I've heard a lot about some Maya Indians here."

"Maya? I thought they disappeared hundreds of years ago."

"Yeah, a lot of people think that. But there are actually a lot of them scattered all over Central America. They just aren't pyramid builders like their ancestors were."

They suddenly heard a loud roar from some place nearby, that sounded like it was up high, it a tree. "What the fuck was that? A jaguar?" Richard asked, stopping and turning toward the sound.

"Nah," Scott said. "That sound I do know. That's a big ol' male Howler Monkey. That's their jaguar imitation, the sound they make when they're trying to scare predators away from their group. He's just telling us to stay away."

"Scared the crap out of me," Richard admitted. "I thought we were fixing to be eaten for sure."

They had only gone a few yards farther when Richard spotted an Indian standing in the middle of the trail through the jungle. But this one didn't have a bow and arrow, or a blow gun. Instead, he carried an old shotgun over his shoulder.

He was short, only a little over five feet tall, extremely muscular with olive colored skin and eyes as black as pitch. His hair was thick and cut evenly, all the way around his head. He was attired in a leather loin cloth and moccasins and had tribal tattoos on his chest. Overall, he was an imposing figure.

"Oh, shit!" Richard said. "Here we go. I hope he's friendly."

They approached the Indian, who seemed to be waiting for them.

"Hi!" Richard offered when they were within a few feet of the Indian.

"Ane, nicca!" the Indian replied.

"Do you, by any chance, speak English?" Richard asked.

At first, the Indian did not respond. Then he shook his head. "Ingles, no. Poquito espanol."

"Let me try," Angie said, and stepped forward. In Spanish, she said, "We need help. We've been in a plane crash. Plane! You know? Large bird that roars."

"The Indian made a sign with his arm like a plane falling.

"Yes, yes! That's right. The bird fell."

"We see bird fall from sky."

"We?" Angie asked. At that moment, a dozen more Indians appeared from the undergrowth, and joined their fellow tribesman on the narrow path. Some were attired in more traditional costumes, which meant very little clothing except for the leather loincloth and moccasins. Some of them carried seven-foot-long blowguns, and pouches which probably held darts.

When they moved, it was as silent as a shadow, although they did not appear to be aggressive. These were children of the forest. They moved silently so they could hunt. They hunted so they could eat.

"Oh shit! What do we do now?" Scott said softly.

Angie waved at the other Indians and continued to speak with Indian number one. His Spanish was limited. It was obvious that he spoke Mayan and perhaps Garifuna, much more than Spanish, which was the only hope Angie had of communicating with him.

"Puede usted ayuda nosotros? (Can you help us?) We need to make it to the beach. La Playa!"

The Indian pointed in the direction of the coast. One of the other Indians stepped forward and unslung a gourd he had been carrying with a lanyard. He took a stopper out and offered it to Angie. She accepted the gourd from the Indian and smiled, saying, "Gracias!"

"Uh oh!" Richard whispered. "You drink whatever is in that gourd and you'll be squirting like a dime store monkey for a month!"

"I've got to take that chance," Angie said. "I think this is their form of a peace offering." Angie held the opening of the gourd up to her lips and sipped the vessel's contents. It was water, and surprisingly cool. She said, "Gracias," and started to hand the gourd back to the Indian, but he motioned for her to pass the gourd around. She nodded, smiled, and handed the gourd to Chelsey.

"Do I want to drink this?" Chelsey asked.

"Just do it," Angie said, "Then hand it to Scott."

Chelsey drank, then handed the vessel across to Scott, who took a deep sip. "That wasn't bad," he said. He wiped his mouth and handed the gourd back to Angie, who handed it to Richard. He, then, drank from the gourd, afterward handed it to the Indian, saying, "Thank you!. Uh, gracias! Did I say that right, Angie?"

"You did fine," she said.

Although communications were sparce, Angie managed to get across to the Indians that she and her friends needed help reaching the coast. Indians offered to help them, but said the trip would take a full day, and invited the survivors to spend the night in their village, then start for the coast the next morning.

"Many cuatro narises," the first Indian said. "Dangerous, travel at night." Angie translated what the Indian said. "Four noses?" Richard said. "What in the duck's tail is a four noses?"

"Fer-de-lance," Angie replied. "Apparently, this part of the jungle is infested with them."

"Oh good!" Richard said. "I was afraid this little safari was going to be boring!"

The survivors agreed that spending the night at the village would be a wonderful idea and were grateful for a safe place to pass the night. Chelsey, in particular, still had vivid memories of the fer-de-lance. A queue was formed, and the survivors were led safely through the jungle along a narrow, almost indiscernible trail to the Indian village, which was almost three miles distant.

By the time they arrived, Chelsey was limping badly from her wounded knee. Some Maya women saw her wound and applied a cloth to the knee, which had been dipped in a brown colored liquid. Chelsey smiled, made an attempt at saying, "Gracias," and held the cloth in place while sitting on a log.

The Maya Indian village was constructed in typical Mayan style. The houses were all arranged in an oval around a central compound area where village activities and events happened. There was also a central fire, which was used for cooking, but at night, logs would be added to raise the flames high for light, so family members could sit close by and tell stories about their day, and watch children play. The smoke from the fire was also an effective mosquito repellent.

This is where the four survivors were led and offered seats on large logs. As weary as they were after what they had been through, the logs felt pretty good.

There was increased activity this afternoon because suddenly, the village was host to four strange visitors in their midst, whom they felt obligated to feed, care for, and entertain. Even here in the jungle there was such a thing as decorum, to say nothing of courtesy and tradition. Indian women chattered and giggled while they cooked, and frequently glanced over at Richard, Scott, Angie and Chelsey as if they were aliens from another world.

"I don't know what they're cooking," Scott said. "But it smells damn good!

"Sure does," Angie said. "I didn't know I was hungry until I got a whiff of whatever it is."

Chelsey pointed to an Indian lady by the cook fire, using a metal lid looking thing for a cooktop. "Oh look. That woman is actually making tortillas, I think!"

"Yeah, well..." Angie said, "It's easier than the commute to the convenience store to buy them pre-made. They have to trek through the jungle, paddle down rivers, fight off a few jaguars. It's just a pain in the ass, so they make them at home."

Chelsey looked over at Angie but said nothing.

The young Indian they had first seen on the path earlier

that day approached Angie, since she was the apparent spokesperson for her group. Not only that, but she was the only one who came close to speaking the Indian's language.

Angie was sitting on a log, so the Indian dropped down on his knees in order to be at eye level with her. He said his name was Cadmael, and he tried to explain to her that the chief of the village, the Cacique, had declared the white people's survival as reason for a celebration. There would be feasting and drinking and dancing traditional dances for their guests' entertainment.

Angie, in turn, told Cadmael that she and her friends were very honored, and asked Cadmael to please thank the Cacique. Cadmael smiled broadly, because he had managed to communicate with this blond lady so well, nodded his head, then he rose and rushed over to the Cacique to relay what had been said. The Cacique smiled and nodded at Angie.

"What was all that?" Richard asked.

"We've been invited to a party," Angie said.

As sundown approached, the shadows grew long from the trees surrounding them, many of which were over one hundred feet tall. For some reason, the children's voices seemed louder as they played, worry free in the compound, surrounded by the stick-wall houses with thatch roofs. Smoke from cook fires curled lazily upward. A plethora of smells from food being prepared gave the entire area a feeling of warmth and security.

By now, all four survivors had traded in their log seats for pads on the ground. Young Indian men stacked large logs on the fire in an 'A' frame design. And the logs took only minutes to ignite. A fire was building that was pushing back the darkness of night, which approached rapidly in the jungle.

The survivors had also been provided with gourds containing drinks...actually, strong drinks, which were the equation of home-made moon shine but made of wild figs instead of corn. The figs contained enough sugar that it was not necessary to add anything else to start the fermentation process.

Angie tipped her gourd back and drank a sip. Wiping her mouth, she said, "The more I think different people live different lives, the more I discover they have in common with us. Even here in the middle of the deepest, darkest jungle, people need to get a little smashed from time to time. Probably, most of the time, just like us!"

Chelsey sipped from her gourd and giggled. "I don't feel the pain in my knee anymore! They ought to patent this stuff!"

Angie held up her gourd and pointed to it, then asked Cadmael in Spanish, "What do you call this stuff?"

"Higada," Cadmael answered, then smiled. "You like?"

"Oh, si! Mucho!" Angie said.

"Me glad," Cadmael said, smiling broadly now. He also turned and told the Cacique what the exchange was about. The Cacique smiled wide and grunted approval. Then he turned his attention back to instructing the women of the village about things to do to prepare for the celebration. All of the women participated, even the ones with small babies. They carried them while they worked, papoose style, in carriers crafted from colorful cloth.

As eventide turned to night, the festivities began. Over two dozen women, all dressed in colorful costumes, emerged from huts to form a circle around the fire. Then, drums sounded a rhythm and small flutes played a tune. The sound was very reminiscent of the music performed by the Inca Indians around Cusco, Peru. The music was very primitive. Angie had no trouble imagining this precise scene happening fifteen hundred years ago.

These were Maya Indians. But Angie wasn't sure which tribe, and for now, it didn't really matter. But the irony was not lost on any of the survivors. "Who would ever believe we would survive a plane crash and wind up at a party... *in the middle of the jungle*, in the same day," Scott said, incredulously. "And get plowed to boot. This fig stuff ain't bad."

"Want to know how they make it?" Angie asked. "Cadmael told me."

Scott thought about it. "I don't think so," he said. "Something tells me I'm better off not knowing."

The drums grew louder, the flutes more melodic, and the heads of the survivors got dizzier. They ate barbequed monkey meat, and didn't care, such was their hunger. There were also yams and tortillas which they feasted on until they were stuffed and drowsy.

The smells of night orchids filled the air with a delicate sweetness. Air that was oxygen rich because of the jungle. They made friends with these children of the forest, and they felt safe from all the worries of the outside world. In this place, and at this time, little else mattered.

They knew that by now they certainly would have been reported missing. People would be worried. A search would have been initiated. But it was nighttime in the jungle. All things of the outside world would have to wait until morning. Right now, they were cocooned, wrapped in a blanket of the night, insulated from the world. And somehow, that was all that mattered, at least for now.

That is, everyone except Ricard. He stared into the flames so intensely that he seemed hypnotized. Angie noticed, even though Richard was sitting on the other side of Scott from her.

"What's up, big guy?" she asked.

"I'm hearing songs in my head," he said. "Songs from many years ago. And those songs are the doorway to too many memories. Not all of them good memories. Memories of how I wronged people in my life. I was so blind... then. Now, it's too late to do anything about it. I can't even beg forgiveness because the ones that are alive don't want to have anything to do with me. And others are dead. Even if they were alive, I don't know how they could ever forgive me. And I can't forgive myself. I don't even know if God will forgive me." Richard sighed a deep sigh, but never blinked; just stared into the fire.

"Time is a real mother-fucker, you know?" Richard lamented. "Why couldn't I have seen the pain I was causing at the time..." Tears found their way down his cheeks. Then he placed his face between his knees and began to sob. His three friends could feel the pain in him. They wanted to console him, but how? You can't forgive somebody if they aren't willing to forgive themselves.

And that is how the night faded into blackness.

CHAPTER NINE

The Rescue

A thousand tree frogs serenaded the survivors to sleep that night. They had been offered the jungle version of a guest house, which was a hut made of sticks for walls, and a thatch roof with mats on the dirt floor to sleep on. Under normal circumstances, none of them would have been able to sleep, or even rest under such primitive conditions. But these circumstances were not normal, and so they were grateful for everything the Indians had done for them, including treat them like honored guests.

Midnight was silent in the jungle, except for the frogs, a few crickets, and the low crackling of the waning fire in the middle of the compound. Sleep came over them all like a warm, comfortable blanket. The stress and exhaustion of the day had caught up to them when they calmed down and managed to feel secure in the Maya village.

They were awakened in the morning by the sound of a helicopter somewhere in the distance. Richard was the first one to hear the sound and respond. He visually searched the horizon above the tree-tops.

"They're searching for us," he said, confidently.

Cadmael came running up to Richard, pointing toward the east. "Machine that flies!" he said in a mixture of Spanish and Mayan. Richard didn't understand his words, but he understood the meaning.

"Si! Si," Richard said excitedly. "Machina!" The excitement was spreading through the village. Now Scott and the ladies were awake.

"What's all the excitement?" Angie asked, rubbing her eyes, trying to get awake.

"Heard a chopper," Richard said enthusiastically. "They're searching for us!"

"Thank God!" Chelsey said, walking up to join the small group.

But although they listened intently, they didn't hear the distant sound of the chopper again for the next few minutes. Instead, the melodic sound of jungle birds flooded in, and some other sounds which Cadmael pointed to and explained that it was a monkey.

Scott joined the group. "So, what do you recommend we do now?"

"I think we should stay right here," Angie said. "If we hit the trail for the coast, we'll be hidden underneath that jungle canopy and they'll never find us. We're in a cleared area here. They are bound to fly over us sooner or later. As little as I know about aerial searches, don't they fly back and forth in an overlapping grid?"

"Yeah," Richard agreed. "If they know what they're doing."

"I'm willing to give them that much credit," Angie said.

There was something else in the air. Something that

made no more noise in flight than an owl. It, too, was searching. It had been to the crash site and found only one body. Frustrated, it wanted to know where the other humans were. It searched the night, peering toward earth through almond-shaped eyes, with elliptical pupils.

The morning was coming to life with the sounds of women chatting as they patted tortillas and cooked them on large, flat metal discs. There was also the smell of beans wafting in the air.

Cadmael approached Angie. In a language that was Spanish, mixed with Mayan and Garifuna, he explained that they should eat before they started for the coast.

"With your kind permission, we want to wait here," Angie explained. "It will be easier for the flying machine to see us here. They are looking for us. They could not see us if we were on the trail."

"Oh!" Cadmael said with a wide smile. He was proud because he managed to understand the blonde woman. He nodded approval, then turned to the Cacique to explain it to him. The Cacique listened, then looked up at the sky. He pointed upward and said something to Cadmael in Mayan. Cadmael went into a deeper explanation While the Cacique listened closely. At the end of the exchange, Cadmael turned to Angie and said. "Cacique say, you stay here, wait for flying machine."

Angie thanked him. The foursome took seats once again on the logs. Chelsey said, "Boy, what I would give for a toothbrush and some toothpaste."

Scott chuckled. "You never know what you've got until it's gone!" Only, he sang the words, like in the song. Then he turned to Richard. "You feeling better this morning?"

"Yeah," Richard said. "Sorry about last night. I'm afraid that fig moonshine got to me. That, and that big, beautiful fire."

"There's no reason to apologize," Scott said. "But I do have an observation, if you don't mind?"

"No. I don't guess so," Richard said, turning to look at Scott.

"Well, you are obviously in a lot of pain. I guess it's just under the surface. But what it sounded to me like is that your conscience is burdening you."

"Yeah, I guess that's right. What's your point?"

"Just this, if you weren't a good soul, a person capable of love, then you wouldn't have a conscience. I think your pain is good news, in a way. It shows ethics. So what if you fucked up years ago? You can't change that. But because of your reaction to it, it will help guide how you treat people today. Maybe you were a turd at one time in your life. But today, I think you're a pretty cool guy!"

Richard thought about Scott's words, then slowly smiled. "I think you're a pretty cool guy too!" Richard said. "And a philosopher. Thank you for that insightful observation. It never occurred to me to think about it that way."

"For what it's worth," Angie interjected. "I completely agree with Scott."

"Me too," Chelsey said.

"Wow!" Richard said. "I couldn't have been in a plane crash with a nicer bunch of people!"

Everybody laughed, just as four village women brought them wooden bowls filled with beans and fresh tortillas. The women handed them the bowls and indicated 'eat' with their hands. "Kekiin," Angie said, the

Mayan word for Thank You. The other survivors thanked them and dug in.

————

Two hours later, breakfast was far behind the survivors. The Belize (or Guatemalan) sun had climbed high into the sky, and it was starting to get hot, especially here. Because in the middle of these tall trees, no breeze can stir, and the humidity is high. Sweating and seeking shade was the order of the day.

"I sure wish I had your camera, to record all of this," Chelsey said to Richard. Richard looked around. He agreed. There was a lot here that it would be nice to document.

Suddenly, Angie said, "You could use my phone to take pictures."

Everybody looked at Angie. "Your phone?" Scott said. "You've got your phone with you?"

"Oh, that's right. I guess it was lost in the crash." Then she reached around and found the phone holster on her belt. There was something in it! Surprised, Angie opened the flap of the holster. Her phone was there, and undamaged!

"Dear God," she said

"What!" everybody said simultaneously.

"Do you have a bar? Even one bar?" Scott wanted to know.

Angie checked. "No. Too far away. Too many trees."

"Too many for a voice call, maybe. But try sending a text."

"Wouldn't that be the same thing?" Angie asked.

"No," Scott said. "Because it goes into a mailbox. I don't know what the difference is, but sometimes you can do that, even when you can't reach somebody with a phone call."

Angie didn't see much use in trying, but she sent a text to Maurine, anyway. "HELP! We've crashed in the jungle south of Placencia. Need rescue." She pressed send.

Nothing! "Well, it was worth a shot," she said, disappointed. Then she handed the phone to Chelsey. "Here, get your pictures. I've still got about 60% battery power left."

Chelsey accepted the phone and began taking pictures of everything she saw. After a few minutes, the phone buzzed.

"Uh oh!" Chelsey said. "I think the battery ran down." She handed the phone back to Angie. Angie checked to see how much battery power there was.

"There's still plenty of battery. Maurine has responded to my text!"

Everybody cheered. Meanwhile, Angie and Maurine began an exchange of texts.

"I've been scared to death! Is everybody alive?"

"Yes, everybody is alright."

"Is Richard okay?"

"Yes, 'A' ok."

"Thank God. How can we find you? How far from the coast are you, or do you know?"

"Twenty or thirty miles. We're safe in a Maya village."

"Really? Does it have a name?"

"Stand by," Angie typed. Then she asked Cadmael, "Cadmael, is your village known by a name?"

"Si. Chan Ba'alam," Cadmael answered proudly.

"Chan Ba'alam," Angie typed into the phone, and hit send.

"Stand by," Maurine said (in text).

Several minutes passed with no more messages. The waiting was torturous. Then, "Air rescue says they know of the village. They are on their way!"

When Angie read the message out loud, everybody cheered and danced around. Angie explained to Cadmael what was going on. The young Indian's reaction was a mixture of excitement and fear.

"The flying machine is coming here?" he wanted to know.

"Yes," Angie said. "They are coming here to pick us up."

"Will they hurt us for helping you?" the Indian wanted to know.

"Of course not. They will show you honor and thank you. You will shine bright in their eyes!"

Cadmael smiled, but then said anxiously, "I must tell the Cacique and the people, so they do not become frightened." He turned and left quickly to find the Cacique.

————

In less than an hour, the sound of a chopper could be heard approaching. Within two minutes, the helicopter was hovering motionless over the village of Chan Ba'alam, and a uniformed man was being lowered to the ground via a cable, with a rescue harness. The villagers looked on in awe. Chelsey was the first person to be strapped into the harness. When it was secure, the uniformed man with Air/Sea Rescue gave a signal, and she was lifted off of the ground, on the way up to the chopper. The harness would be returned in a minute for Angie.

She went to Cadmael and thanked him warmly for everything he and the villagers had done to help them. Cadmael smiled and said something. But the noise from the chopper was too loud, and Angie didn't hear him. Instead, she patted him on the shoulder and rushed to the spot where she would be strapped into the harness. Then she waved goodbye one last time when the cable tightened and lifted her off the ground. She saw Cadmael talking to the Cacique and pointing to the chopper but could not hear their conversation.

Minutes later, Scott and Richard were on board, and then the Air/Sea Rescue member was hauled up, the bay door was closed, and they were on their way to civilization and safety.

CHAPTER TEN

The Conundrum

"What are you going to do now?" Maurine sat at a large round table in the restaurant at Robert's Grove Resort with Angie, Chelsey, Scott, James, Al and Richard, who sat to Maurine's right.

Angie looked very deep in thought. "Don't know. As bad as I hate to admit it, we're right back where we started. I've made no progress at all," Angie said, so softly that it almost sounded like a whisper. "This bitch is smarter than her sister, or she learned lessons from watching her sister... something. Whatever the reason, she's more dangerous.

"It's a wonder we're alive! If it hadn't been for Niles handling that plane as well as he did, we would all be shish-kabobs right now, just like he is. Poor bastard!"

"What happened out there?" Maurine asked.

'We were headed back this way, after surveying the Blue Hole," Angie said, almost in a trance. "Something slammed against the plane, hard. Screwed up some of the steering stuff. Made the plane go off to the left, and we started losing altitude. Niles did everything he could to correct course and elevation, but there was too much damage. Tried to call for help. Radio was out. I think he wanted to ditch in the water just off the beach, but he had no control, or damned little. We kept losing altitude. He found a clearing in the jungle and pulled the plug. Then the clearing turned out to be full of tree stumps. That made for a rough landing and poor Niles took a big splinter in the throat. He gave his life to save ours."

"Yes, well, he had one thing in common with Henry," Maurine said, sadness in her voice. "He was married and had kids."

"Oh, shit! Does his wife know yet?"

"I'm not sure. I'll check on it," Maurine said. Then she looked at Richard. "The party is getting kind of rough. Are you still sure you want to be a part of it?"

"More than ever," Richard said.

"Could be dangerous."

"I'm counting on it!" Richard said, with a smile.

How could Maurine confess to Richard that when they were missing, she was worried, and scared to death that something might have happened to him? Here was a man who was brave and the courage wasn't alcohol induced. It was...genuine!

"Angie tells me you pinned a snake's head, picked it up and moved it away from the plane without killing it."

"Yes, that's right. I saw no reason to kill it," Richard said. "After all, we were in the snake's living-room, guests, as it were. To have killed it would have been a little bit like a home invasion." Richard smiled.

"What kind of snake was it?"

"I believe it was a fer-de-lance."

"Oh, good Lord," Maurine said. "Those things are very deadly!"

"Yes, they are. But that doesn't change the facts any. The snake was minding its own business, in the jungle. We came there. He didn't invite us. If he would have been in my living-room, the situation, and response, might have been different. Why is this an issue? All's well that ends well. I happen to believe that animals have the right to live too. It's very narcissistic to assume human beings are superior and have preferential rights on this planet. We have to share it with creatures."

So then, how do you feel about the siren, or her sister, whatever she is?"

"She's a danger. She's killing people. All bets are off. She has to go. I don't see how that applies here. It's a totally different situation."

"Yes, I agree," Maurine said. I'm just glad we're on the same page."

"Now all we have to do is find her, and then kill her. Not quite that easy, is it?"

Everybody looked at Angie. She took a deep drink of her Siren's potion, sat it down and said, "I want to go back out to the ranch tomorrow. It's a long shot, but at this point, I'm desperate."

Maurine looked at her quizzically but didn't say anything. Angie caught the look. "When we were trying to corner Maris, I got a little help from some ancient spirits. I doubt that she will show up again, but we've got to take the chance. It's all we've got."

"The ranch?" Chelsey asked. "Can I go?"

"Yeah, just so long as you keep your mouth shut if the old broad shows up."

"I promise!" Chelsey said.

"You said 'spirits', as in plural," Maurine said, quizzically.

Angie paused a minute before speaking. "Yeah... about that. Remember Dimitri?"

"Yes, of course."

"Well, he wasn't who he seemed on the surface."

Scott, overhearing Angie talk about Dimitri, started turning red in the face. So, he got up and walked out of the restaurant. Angie watched him go, then groaned. "Oh crap! That was bad timing!"

———

The next morning found the Robert's Grove Resort SUV, bouncing down the old dirt 'ranch road' on the way to the 'Robert's Getaway' Ranch. Tontoni was the chauffeur for three passengers, Angie, Chelsey, and Richard. It had been decided that Scott, James and Al would stay at the resort. Too many people present at the ranch might discourage an appearance. And Angie needed very much for 'the old broad' to show up to the party!

When they arrived, Tontoni pulled into the parking area and stopped, killed the motor, and unwrapped a stick of gum to chew while he waited on the three Americans to complete their mission. Hopefully, on a positive note.

Angie used the key that Maurine had provided to open the front door. Just as the last time she was here, the house smelled slightly musty. So, she went straight to the thermostat and turned on the AC. Then she found a can of Lysol and sprayed all over the house to chase the odor.

After that, she went to the library and began looking for the old book entitled, 'FOLKLORE OF THE CARIBBEAN'.

She found it in exactly the same place she remembered leaving it. "Jesus!" she said, as she paged through the book, looking for the chapter about Maris. "De Ja Vous! Been here, done this. How in the world do I keep winding up here?"

Angie found the passage that mentioned Maris's sister, but just as she remembered and suspected, there was nothing that would be of any help. She pushed the book away from her, toward the middle of the table. Richard pulled it toward himself and began leafing through the volume.

Thirty minutes later, he commented, "It's interesting how much stuff there is in here about sea spirits, and sudden storms, to say nothing of the fascinating passage about this siren that you say was called Maris."

"Yeah. Makes you wonder where the author got all of his information," Angie said as she looked around for any other text that might help them. There just was nothing. It was frustrating to Angie because information was what she needed. Her life, and the lives of many people, depended on it.

Three hours later, Richard was deep into the book. Chelsey had found something else to read and was making notes. Angie slouched slightly in a chair with her fingers interlocked and her eyes closed, taking a nap. Faintly, from outside, a radio could be heard playing. Tontoni had the van radio turned on to some reggae music. Bob Marley was singing about how he shot the sheriff, but not the deputy.

A voice penetrated Angie's slumber. A female voice that Angie somehow recognized. "This one flies," the voice said. Angie was suddenly awake. She opened her eyes and there, sitting in the chair next to her was the old woman, still dressed in gossamer robes of black, just like the last time they had met. Richard and Chelsey looked up from what they had been doing at the sound of the voice. They were stunned. Neither of them had observed the old woman enter the library.

She looked at Angie, as she said, "She cannot be killed on the ground, or even in the water. She must be killed in the air, which is her domain. And you must use the same obsidian dagger that was used to kill her sister, the very same one."

"What else?" Angie asked, her attention riveted on the old woman.

"You must tell her a lie moments before you kill her. It must be a lie that confuses her."

"A lie?" Angie said. "About what?"

"You will know when the time comes," the old woman said, almost smiling. Then she turned to Chelsey and Richard. She smiled a wrinkled smile and said to both of them, "I'll see you soon!" Then, she rose from her chair and left the library, turning left into the hallway. Richard quickly jumped up to follow the old woman.

"Don't bother," Angie admonished. "She's gone. That's her version of 'exit, stage left'."

Richard made it to the hallway, looked left, but true to Angie's words, the hallway was empty.

"What the barbequed hell was that?" Richard demanded. "'See you soon!' How is she going to see me soon?"

"I was wondering that myself," Chelsey said. "That's kinda scary! Angie, what did she mean?"

"Don't ask me," Angie said, rising from her chair. "I know less now than when I started this frigging snipe hunt!" She headed out of the library, en route to the front door. "Come on, let's get the hell out of here! We accomplished our mission, such as it was!"

When they were all getting into the van, Tontoni started the motor and then asked, "You give up?"

"No," Angie replied. "We saw her."

"Saw who?" Tontoni asked.

"The old woman. Didn't she just leave?"

"Ain't nobody left here. Nobody came, nobody left, 'cept for you people." Tontoni looked at them, a little puzzled.

Angie nodded. "Okay, Tontoni, let's blow this pop stand!"

Richard rolled his head back as the van left the parking area. "This has been the wildest few days of my entire life. When you first told me the story, I have to admit, I took it with a grain of salt. You know, two thousand year old sirens, spirits that you talk to like they were your next door neighbor. I guess it just didn't sink in. But now... that old woman who we just had a brief meeting with... No! An 'encounter' with was..."

"A spirit," Angie finished.

"Incredible," Richard said. "Just freaking incredible! I mean, I just..." He fell silent. There was a mirror attached to the back side of the sun visor on the passenger side of the vehicle. Angie used it to look back at Richard, who now stared out the window at the lowland jungle, as they passed by, bouncing along, en route back to Robert's Grove Resort.

"Do you know what a conundrum is?" Richard asked, as he looked into the mirror, so he could see Angie's face.

"I'm of the impression that it has a handful of definitions," Angie said.

"Okay then," Richard said. "We have a handful of conundrums. I would say the first one is, what does this person, or thing, look like? It's a whole lot easier to gear up for battle if you know what you're battling looks like. Right now, I feel like I'm fixing to take on the endoparasitoid from 'Alien'."

"You may not be far from right," Angie said, solemnly. "I'd like to know what this broad looks like myself! Endo... what? How did you memorize that long word?"

Richard smiled. "I was fascinated with that whole series of movies. It was definitely Sigourney Weaver's finest hour. You know? I call it fitting in the right slot. Like, James Arness was born to play Matt Dillon. Sigourney Weaver was born to play Ridley."

"I guess if that's the case, I was born to be a siren hunter, although it's the last thing I ever expected to be. Or for that matter... want to be!"

"Sometimes fate plays a hand in things like this," Chelsey offered.

"Fate?" Angie said. "God help me. That is too scary to even consider! That hints of preordination. I would hate to think that somebody other than me is steering my ship! I have enough trouble keeping it off the reef, without any outside 'help'!"

———

Later that afternoon, Maurine approached Richard, who was standing on the deck of the beachside bar, watching a man in a small boat, anchored just offshore, cleaning lobsters and dropping the unwanted parts overboard. Maurine saw what he was looking at.

"We've bought all of his lobsters for a lobster cookout tonight on the beach. You coming?"

"Wouldn't miss it!" Richard said. "This place grows on you, and it doesn't take long to do it."

"Really? I'm glad you feel that way, because there's something I'd like to talk to you about," Maurine said.

"Oh? What's that?"

"Well, as laid back as things usually are here, we've had a few incidents lately that give me concern. I think we would be wise to have a security person on staff." She watched closely, waiting to see his reaction. After a minute, she continued.

"Obviously, that wouldn't be a full-time job. At least, let's hope not. So, I was thinking, we could also use a liaison, a person to assist tourists when they have little particular problems. I constantly have people come into the office with some knit picking something-or-other they need help with. I don't mind, except that it distracts me from what I'm supposed to be doing. And my partner, Michael, is doing quite a bit of traveling these days."

"What kind of knit-picking things are you talking about?"

"Oh, a good example is, this lady wanted to go into town the other day to look for some medicine. It was a prescription medication, but she had left her bottle at home and really needed the pills. I had to get an appointment for her with Doc. He examined her and gave her the prescription, but then she had to go to the pharmacy and get it filled. Things like that. I had to assist her with all of that, and like I say, I don't mind. But it keeps me from getting other things done. If I had a guest liaison..."

"He could intervene. Divert. Assist with some things like that?"

"Exactly. And that's just one example. All sorts of things crop up."

"Very interesting. What kind of deal are you offering?"

"Well, that's negotiable. But certainly, a place to live, and food. You would have laundry service, transportation at your disposal anytime. Salary on top of that. You won't get rich, but you will live well. You can go diving or deep sea fishing anytime you like."

"Damn! That isn't a job, it's a paid vacation!"

"Oh, you'll earn your pay. I'm not in the habit of giving away money."

Richard smiled.

Maurine looked at him. "Well, you interested?"

"Of course! Only an idiot wouldn't be. I think you have a deal. But I also think it would be best to not set our deal into motion until this thing with Angie is resolved, one way or the other."

"Okay, I can understand that. I'll do all the paperwork to bring you on board, but we won't sign it until 'whatever it is' has reached a conclusion."

"Done," Richard said. Maurine shook his hand and walked away, with Dolly at her side, a special perkiness in her stride. Her body language indicated that she was very happy.

————

Meanwhile, Scott, Al Harmon and James Harmon were pulling up to the dock in a large fishing boat for which they had pitched in together and hired to take them fishing. They looked tired, but happy as they climbed onto the pier, then offloaded a large red cooler that looked heavy with the day's catch. Al grabbed the handle on one end of the cooler, James got the other. Scott brought up the rear. They walked toward the restaurant toting their load. As they passed by Maurine, they smiled and bragged, "Robalo and red snapper!" Al said proudly. "We're gonna feast tonight!"

"But we're having a lobster barbeque on the beach tonight," Maurine said.

"Really?" Al said. "Well... we'll work it out somehow. Maybe a giant fish fry tomorrow night! How's that sound?"

"Parteeeee!" Maurine said, laughing. She was in a decidedly good mood.

Angie & Chelsey had been walking on the beach some distance from the resort. Chelsey had a small voice recorder in her hand. It appeared she was interviewing Angie. Chelsey had earned Angie's trust enough by now, especially after having endured the experience in the jungle.

But Angie, seeing that Scott was returning from his fishing trip, broke off her visit with Chelsey, so that she could join Scott.

"Did you catch a lot?" Angie asked.

"Oh man, did we!" Scott answered. That water out there

is roiling with fish. And our guide knew exactly where to take us. I caught a robalo... I mean, snook, almost three feet long. That is one of the best eating kinds of fish. And then we went into deeper water and caught snapper. Oh man! We are going to have such a feast"

"We all like to eat fish. There's no question about that. But there's a lobster barbeque on the beach tonight."

"Yeah, I heard. That isn't a problem. The cooks will clean our catch and ice it down for tomorrow. But right now, I need a shower that will last about thirty minutes, then a little nap, with you, hopefully. Then clean clothes, and on to the party on the beach!"

Angie smiled. "I think a nap can be arranged. As for the shower, I need one too. Why don't we just do it together?"

"I like your thinking," Scott said.

————

Minutes later, Scott and Angie were in the shower together, washing each other's bodies. As they did so, nature took its course. Scott became aroused, Angie aided and abetted. She took his manhood in her soapy hands and worked gently, making sure he was very, very clean!

Scott responded by taking her in his arms and there, with warm water cascading over them, he kissed her deeply, passionately, lovingly. Angie's desire for her man came fully awake. She took his hand and led him from the shower, stopping long enough to give him a cursory drying with a large, fluffy towel. Then she placed the towel between them and rubbed herself against him.

"You're driving me crazy!" Scott said.

"Good," Angie said, smiling. "Then my plan is working."

"Plan?"

"Yes. It's a very simple plan, Mr. Clouseau. You lie down on the bed and I will sexually assault you!"

"That's my kind of plan," Scott said, falling back on the bed, dropping the oversized towel on the floor. Then, perfectly built Angie climbed on top of Scott and made good her threat to vanquish him. She took Scott inside of her and kept him there for the better part of an hour while she moved slowly, sensuously, expertly. Scott moved too. Joining Angie, matching her speed and thrust. At last, they both became very vocal as an explosion of equally timed orgasms sent shock waves through their bodies.

By the time she stopped, they were both sated and exhausted. She raised up so she could take him out of her, rolled to the left and fell beside him, then drifted off into a beautiful, peaceful slumber, safe in the arms of the man she loved. Within moments, Scott joined her in sleep, his arms wrapped tightly around this amazing woman. He was joyous, at peace, but also sad. What if she found out?

———

Loud music awakened Scott and Angie. It was coming from somewhere in the distance. The gentle sea breeze carried it right into their room. They quickly got out of bed and dressed, then exited their sanctuary to see where the joyful noise was coming from.

They were surprised to see that evening was nigh. It was eventide, and the party had started on the beach. The smells of good cooking over an open fire were in the air.

The sea breeze brought both the sounds and smells to them.

"Ohh, this looks like fun!" Angie said, moving slightly to the music as she walked, side by side with Scott. Scott brought his camera, hoping to capture a few good stills of the revelry around the fire.

As they approached, they saw that everyone else had assembled where the action was happening before they did. Chelsey was there, chatting with Maurine. Faithful Dolly was at Maurine's side. Al, James and Richard had managed to find folding chairs to sit in and were enjoying relaxed conversation while holding onto cold beers. The main topic was the exciting fishing day they had experienced.

"Did you see that damned sea turtle?"

"Yeah. I thought he sumbitch going to ask us for a beer!"

"Nah! The sumbitch wanted my robalo. I do the work, the turtle gets to eat the sushi!" They laughed. Al was first to look up and see Angie and Scott. "Hey there! Welcome to the hoe-down," Al said. "There are some more folding chairs over there, or there are some driftwood logs to sit on. Whatever suits your fancy."

"Before I do anything else," Scott said. "I need one of those beers!"

Al pointed to a large picnic table. "There's a cooler over there with three or four kinds, and lots of them! Go for it!"

Angie stood there, arms crossed, looking up at the moon. "Looks like it's going to be a full, bright one tonight," she said to Maurine.

"That's the reason we chose tonight for this shindig," Maurine said.

Other resort guests were all sitting around the fire,

waiting for it to get completely dark. They were drinking, laughing, relaxing, having a good time. Somebody on the other side of the fire said something humorous, and several people laughed.

"This is nice, you know?" Richard said. "I don't think I have ever sat around a campfire like this, the smell of woodsmoke in the air, to say nothing of the smell of lobsters barbequing... Well, there was the other night. The Indians cooking monkey meat. Strange, but that smelled great too, and tasted great." Then he turned to Maurine. "I've had time to think about our deal quite a bit. I am grateful. I am going to enjoy this assignment."

"What assignment is that?" Angie asked. So, Maurine and Richard both told her what they had planned. First one, then the other, would speak. By the time they had finished, Angie was opened mouthed with joy. "Oh my God! That is so terrific! Congratulations to you, Richard! And Maurine, smart move! Very smart!"

Then, when things had settled down a little, Angie wandered over next to Maurine with her back to Richard and said softly, out of the corner of her mouth to Maurine, "So what's really going on? Are you falling for this guy?"

"If I was, would that be such a bad thing?" Maurine asked.

"Answering a question with a question is always a give-away!" Angie said, ever so softly. "Well, good luck. He seems like a nice guy, and you certainly deserve some happiness. All you do is work, work, work, sixteen, eighteen hours per day!"

Maurine just smiled, then took a sip of her drink.

Meanwhile, Scott had managed to find a flat place atop

a log to park his beer for a minute. So, he was busy with his camera, finding interesting shots to take. It occurred to him to get back a few yards from the fire. In fact, he worked his way around behind the group of revelers to take a photo, so they would be in silhouette. He got very lucky with that picture; the silhouetted party-going resort guests, laughing and being animated, then the bonfire beyond them, flames licking the air, smoke curling upward. Then, on the opposite side of the fire, there was his own party of people, sitting talking, waiting for the lobster to be cooked to a turn. The firelight shined on their faces, making this a perfectly balanced photo.

All in all, it was a photographic version of a Norman Rockwell painting. Except that this was not Americana. It was Belize. Well, maybe Americana, because these were Americans, for the most part, in the picture. Whatever! Scott found himself inspired and took over a hundred pictures by the time he slowed down and retrieved his beer, which was now a little warm. He didn't care. The photo op had been worth it.

To complete the picture, somebody showed up with a guitar. Somebody that knew how to use it. Soft music emanated from the guitar to perfectly complement the atmosphere.

The evening was textbook. There was laughter, eating fine food, more laughter, some drinking, yes, but nobody got sloppy. After dinner, a few couples decided to take a short stroll down the beach and take advantage of the moonlight. The evening breeze was very light. The waves washing up on the beach were very small and lazy, completing the romantic picture.

Scott and Angie decided to follow the example of other people who had strolled down the beach. So, hand in hand, they walked in the moonlight, slowly, chatting about nothing in particular, pushing aside all the reasons Angie had come here in the first place. Somehow, that was 'somewhere else' for the moment. The world was right here, right now.

They heard voices coming from behind them that sounded familiar. They stopped and looked back to see Richard and Maurine following everyone else's example about taking a walk in the moonlight. They were about fifty yards behind Scott and Angie.

Angie looked up at the perfectly round moon. "Moon is really bright tonight, huh?"

"Yeah," Scott said. "I think this is the summer solstice."

"Oh. That's nice. Bright light, though. Bright enough that I think I can see a romance blooming!"

"I kind of figured you were going to say that," Scott said, walking along, looking out at the moonlit water.

———

It was almost 2:00 a.m. by the time Scott and Angie got back to their room, tired and very happy. They both yawned wide and began undressing, ready for a night of snuggling and sleeping, and perhaps dreaming pleasant dreams. Then it happened.

Scott had taken his shirt off and tossed it on a chair. Something near the collar caught Angie's attention. She walked to the chair and picked up the shirt to inspect it.

"Scott, is this one of the shirts you had with you when you went to South Texas?"

Scott looked over to where Angie stood with the shirt in her hands. "Yeah. It's dirty, but I didn't take time to wash clothes when I got back. I felt like I needed to get down here to you as quickly as possible. Why?"

"A little bit careless, weren't you?" She showed the red smudge to Scott. He looked at it, then tried to toss it off.

"That's nothing. They had a big wrap party when I finished. Those people love to party more than we do," Scott said, laughing as he talked, then catching a sideways glance at Angie.

"What was her name?" Angie asked.

"What? Who? Oh, the lipstick lady? To be honest, I'm not sure. There were a lot of cowgirls at that party, all acting as wild as the Texas wind! You know!" More nervous laughter.

"I said, what was her fucking name, Scott? Now tell me the truth."

"Pearl," Scott said, dropping his pretense. He knew he had been caught.

"Hmmm! 'Pearl'! Now ain't that jes down home fancy, y'all! Tell me, Scott, does 'Pearrrrlll' know how to suck a dick as well as I do? Does she know how to take it inside her and wrap her legs around you the way I do? Huh? Tell me. What about the way she kisses?"

"It just happened," Scott pleaded. "I got a little drunk at the party..."

"A 'little' drunk? You must have been out of your fucking mind, knee crawling blasted, you sonofabitch! Tell me, how did it happen? Did you go to her place? A motel? Your motel room? Where, you mother fucker? Where?"

"In a horse barn."

"What? Oh, that must have been romantic! The delicate fragrance of horse shit was in the air! The perfume-like aroma seduced you! You fucking cur dog! Not only did you cheat on me, you rutted like an animal!"

By now, Angie was screaming. She grabbed Scott's suitcase and headed for the door, opened it and threw the suitcase as far out the door and she could, and the shirt after it. "Yippy-kai-yea, you piece of shit!" She shrieked.

"But where am I supposed to sleep?" Scott pleaded.

"I don't know. It's an interesting topic for discussion, but not in my bed. Get the fuck out of this room, right now!"

Scott, shoulders slumped, looking like a whipped dog, walked out the door. Angie slammed it as hard as she could behind him. So hard that she woke up a couple of guests in other rooms with the noise and vibration.

CHAPTER ELEVEN

Where Is Scott?

Angie spent half the night alternating between being furious and crying. Finally, sleep took her blissfully away from her angst and despair and gave her peace. She awoke the next morning when someone knocked on her door. She thought it was Scott. She went to the door, sleepy eyed, ready to forgive him, now that her tantrum had passed, But, that was not the case.

To her surprise, when she opened the door, Tontoni was standing there with Scott's suitcase in his hand. "This belong to you, Miss?"

Bleary-eyed, Angie looked at the suitcase. "Yeah, that's my boyfriend's suitcase. Where's you find it?"

"Just over there a few feet," Tontoni said, pointing over his shoulder.

"Oh! Well, bring it in, please. Just put it there, on the suitcase rack." Tontoni quickly complied. Angie thanked him and he left.

After Tontoni had gone, Angie went into the bathroom to brush her teeth and do other basic toilette, so that she could get put together enough to go to the restaurant for breakfast. But the question kept nagging her; why had Scott gone off and left his suitcase lying on the walkway outside the room? Anyone could have come along and gotten it. He was lucky it was Tontoni who had found it.

Then another thought occurred to her. *Oh my God! What if Maris's sister had seen him leave the room? What if she had seized on his moment of vulnerability? Was he lying dead somewhere, half eaten by.... Her?* With an utterance of, "Oh Jesus!" Angie scrambled to get into some clothes and sprinted out the door.

She found Maurine sitting in the restaurant, sipping coffee and going over some papers. Angie ran up to her and plopped down in a chair. "Scott is missing!"

"What?" Maurine said, as she looked up from her papers.

"Scott is missing," Angie repeated, breathlessly. "We had a fight last night when we came back to the room. I kicked him out. Threw his suitcase out the door. Tontoni found it this morning in the same place where I had thrown it. Did you by any chance put him in another room for the night?"

"No. I haven't seen him," Maurine said. She motioned to one of the waiters. When he came to the table, she said, "One of our guests is missing. Would you round up a couple of men and look for him? It's Scott Carrington. You've seen him. He's Angie's boyfriend."

"Yes Ma'am, right away!" the waiter responded, and quickly left the table. Turning back to Angie, Maurine said, "What did you fight about?"

"Oh, well..." Angie said, hesitantly. "It seems that Scott made a slip-up while he was in South Texas."

"Made a slip-up? That word usually translates to fooled around."

"Yeah, that one," Angie admitted.

"And you kicked him out for it?" Maurine said, one eyebrow going up.

"Yeah, I lost it. I think it was the liquor."

"Um hum. Correct me if I'm wrong, but didn't you do something a little similar the last time you were down here?"

"How did you know about that?"

"Oh, come on!" Maurine said, laughing. "You got hammered right out there on the deck, in front of three dozen people, including reporters, and started talking about fellatio with 'the biggest rod in Belize'! At the top of your voice, I might add!"

"Oh... that!"

"Yeah, that. I'm not saying what Scott did was right, by any means. But you might want to ease up on him just a little. That is, in consideration of the old Biblical saying."

"What saying?"

"The one about the person without sin being the first one to cast a stone.. something like that."

"Oh, yeah... that one!"

"Not too many stones laying around in here!"

"Nope. Point taken."

"Good. Now let's have breakfast while the men look for your lost lover."

"But he might..."

"What?"

"Maris's sister."

"Oh, take a chill pill! Has anything happened around

here? She's out at the Blue Hole. She doesn't give a damn about Robert's Grove. They'll find Scott passed out somewhere, most likely on the beach. He'll show up here, hat in hand. You two will kiss and make up. Happy ending! All's well that ends well!"

"It's really that simple to you, isn't it?"

"This isn't my first time at the rodeo, dearie!" Maurine said, like a wise professor.

Just at that moment, Richard walked in, followed closely by James and Al Harmon. Seeing the two women at the table, they joined them.

"Good morning, ladies," Richard said with a wide smile. "Everybody sleep well?"

"Not Angie," Maurine said as she took a sip of her coffee.

"Uh oh! Why not?" Richard asked, looking at Angie.

"She and Scott had a lover's spat," Maurine volunteered.

"Maurine!" Angie admonished.

"What?" Maurine said. "It'll be all over Placencia by the end of the day, anyway. There's no way to keep secrets in a place like this."

"So, what happened?" Al asked. "You kick his ass out?"

"Yes," Angie admitted. "Now, that is, this morning, his suitcase was found in the same place where I threw it last night. But he's nowhere around."

"Hmm!" James said. "Think we ought to go looking for him?"

"I've already sent some men," Maurine said, as a huge bowl of fruit arrived at the table. "If they don't find him in an hour or so, I'll expand the search. I doubt if he got much farther than one of those palapa bars on the beach."

"What? You think he might have wound up shacking up with some palapa bar floozie?" Angie asked, now with renewed alarm.

"Angie!" Maurine said. "You threw the man out! He had no place to stay. He was obviously in despair. There's no telling what kind of crap he's gotten himself into. He's a man! We all know men don't use the best judgement in a time like that."

"Hey!" Al protested. "Not all men are the same. That's like saying that all women are the same."

"Really?" Maurine said. "You ever gotten crossways with your wife? Enough that you left the house?"

"Well, yeah," Al confessed. "It was years ago, but yeah. Once... I think."

"And what did you do when you 'left the house'?"

"Best I remember, I went some place and got drunk."

"I rest my case!" Maurine said triumphantly.

At that moment, the walkie talkie that Maurine had in a holder on her belt crackled to life. "Robert's Grove," she said into the walkie talkie.

"This be Kenneth," the voice came back. "I be walking on the beach to the south. I've come at least two kilometers. Nothing yet, but I'm still looking."

"Thank you, Kenneth," Maurine answered.

The walkie crackled again. "Irvin here. I'm headed north, along the beach, looking in all the palapa bars. Nobody seen him along here!"

"Thank you, Irvin," Maurine said. She placed the walkie talkie back in her belt holder. "I still have trouble believing Scott got himself in any real trouble. But who knows? Maybe! Anyway, let's finish breakfast. If nothing of a miracle nature happens by then, we'll go to level two."

"What's level two?"

"Intensify and expand. Get the local fuzz involved if need be. They need something to do, anyway. There isn't that much excitement around here."

Angie felt perplexed. She wanted to search, but she didn't know where. It seemed that Maurine had things perfectly organized. So, after breakfast, she went back to her room to use the restroom, and just be by herself for a while. She was really feeling guilty. She shouldn't have blown up like that. It's just that, only a few hours before the ugly truth surfaced, she and Scott had made such sweet love. And then, to find out there had been betrayal, just blind-sided her, caught her off balance. So, she blew!

Because she could think of nothing else to do, she started to lie back on the bed and think for a little while. Maybe come up with her own plan. That's when she noticed Scott's camera on the night table, where he had placed it when they came back to the room last night. She sat on the bed and picked up the camera, turned it on and opened up the shot-check window to see what pictures he had captured.

There were dozens of pictures of the beach party. All of them were, as expected, very good shots. Scott was an excellent photographer. Then one picture caught her eye. The shot check screen was very small, so she had to squint to see everything. The picture was taken from behind all of the party guests, seen in silhouette because of the campfire. Everything looked normal at first. Then she looked closer at the image of a female on the left side of the partiers. At first, she seemed to be one of them. But a closer look showed that she had wings! Wings!

Why the hell hadn't anybody seen wings while she was there in person? Was no one looking that closely? Did this creature have the ability of mass hypnosis? Were those fucking wings just not visible to the naked eye?

Angie was off of the bed in a heartbeat, camera in hand, headed out the door. She found Maurine in the office, behind the reception desk. Angie quickly approached the desk. She turned the camera so the shot check window was facing Maurine.

"Look! See anything unusual? Remember when Dolly was growling last night and we couldn't understand why? Always trust your dog!"

Maurine accepted the camera from Angie and studied the image for a minute. At first, she didn't notice anything unusual, looked up at Angie, and shrugged. "Look again." Andie insisted. Maurine took a second look. "On the left side," Angie said. Maurine refocused. Then, "Oh crap!" She was on the phone within seconds, and within minutes, there was a chopper sitting down on the beach in front of Robert's Grove Resort. Richard, Al, James, Maurine and Angie climbed on board, and the helicopter was airborne.

"Fly in circles," Richard instructed the pilot. "Start tight, then slowly work your way out with each revolution."

Maurine was on the phone, arranging for a police search. All others on board were looking out windows, searching for anything at all unusual.

But after an hour of being airborne, they had seen nothing. Oh, there had been lots of tourist sights—pods of manatees, some giant manta rays schooling around some small fish they were feeding on. Even some sharks, easily seen in the clear water. But no sign of a lone person hiking on the beach, or, God forbid, a body. They decided to return to the resort and wait for a police report.

When the chopper landed on the beach in front of the resort, Angie squinted and thought she recognized Scott, sitting at a table on the deck, a drink in his hand. Yes! It was him. By now, Angie didn't know how to react. She was relieved to see him alive, but furious at the same time. Where the hell had he been?

As they got down from the helicopter and walked toward Scott, Maurine and Angie glanced at each other, puzzled. Al, upon spotting Scott, said, "Well, kiss my ass!" Other comments were made as the group approached the table. Scott wasn't sure what to think. He was looking like death warmed over.

Angie stopped at the table but did not sit. "Where have you been?" she demanded.

"Asleep, in the Dorado," he said, meekly.

"The Dorado? The resort fishing boat?"

"Yeah. After you kicked me out last night, I didn't have any place to go. I went in the bar and got a bottle, took it to the boat and drank myself into oblivion. I just woke up a little while ago. I feel like I've been eaten by a billy goat and shit over a cliff. Where have you all been?"

"Looking for your miserable ass," Angie replied. "We've been all the way up and down that coast, trying to see if your body might be floating up onto the beach. The cops are out looking for you."

"Oh my God!" Maurine said. "That reminds me. I've got

to call off the dogs!" She grabbed her cell phone and walked away, toward the office.

Richard started chuckling. "We should probably go. You two have plenty to talk about, and don't need our help! Come on, guys. I think we all need a pick-me-upper." As they started to walk away, James said, "Me too?"

"You're too young, and you know it, fart blossom!" Al said.

Angie looked squarely at Scott.

He felt her eyes boring into him. "What?" he finally said.

"I'm just waiting," she answered.

"For what? For me to say I'm sorry? I am sorry. It was a stupid thing to do. To be honest, I don't even know how it happened. I was drinking tequila Jell-O shots. They hit me like a hammer. I was smashed. I mean, *really* smashed! I know that's no excuse. I'm not trying to use it for one. But... I do think it was a contributor."

"How many times did it happen?"

"Just once. I swear by all that is holy. Once. When I woke up the next morning, I felt deeply ashamed."

"Did she spend the night with you?"

"No. It was in the horse barn, not even in a bed. If you will forgive me and take me back, I swear to you with all that I am, it will never happen again. I love you, Angie. Please, don't let me lose you over one fuck up. We have too much going to let one stupid..." Scott paused, his voice catching. ".. and it didn't mean anything. It's not like it was an 'affair,' that happened multiple times."

"Why don't you shut up, Scott, while you're still ahead?"

Scott clammed up and, still looking meek, stared imploringly at Angie.

"Okay, this is going to be the way it is," Angie said. "I'll give you one more chance. But if you ever fuck around on me again, not only will I leave you for good, I'll kick you in the groin so hard that you'll be using your balls for a hat. Is that understood and agreed?

"Yes," Scott said.

Angie started to walk away from the table. "You need to get cleaned up. You look like shit, and smell kind of like it, too."

After she walked a few feet, she heard Scott say, "So what about you?"

She stopped. "What?"

"Does that rule about faithfulness apply to you, too?"

"Of course. Why would you say that?"

"Oh, I heard some rumors about the last time you were down here."

Angie went cold. She hesitated several moments before asking, "How long have you known?"

"A long time," Scott said, softly. Angie felt weak. She had just put Scott through hell for doing the same thing she had done to him first.

"Why didn't you ever say something before now?"

"Because I love you. I knew that you were up against a lot down here, and I just didn't see anything to be gained by adding to your problems."

She heard Scott's words, and it made her shut her eyes tight in an attempt to push the pain away. There was nothing she could think of to say in this moment, so she continued to walk away, toward the room. She felt slightly nauseous and definitely weak in the knees. But she made it. She was scared to death Scott would say something else, and if he did, she had no response. Luckily, he had said all that he wanted to say. It's all that was needed to make Angie feel two inches high.

CHAPTER TWELVE

We Need A Plan!

A ngie made it as far as the bar/restaurant, but she needed food, and most of all, she needed something to drink. Maurine was there with Dolly. Angie walked in, sat down, and whistled for the dog.

"Come here, pooch! I need to hold you for a minute. I miss my Pulga, back home. I wish she was down here with me. You two would be great friends, I just know you would!"

"How are things with you and Scott?" Maurine asked.

"We have decided to let bygones be bygones," Angie said as she snuggled the dog.

"Uh oh! So, he knows about last year?"

"How did you get that from, let bygones be bygones?"

"Plural statement. Usually implies that more than one person is in the soup!"

"Um. Well, yeah, you're right. Big difference is, he is a lot more benevolent about it than I am... was. He made me feel two inches tall without ever raising his voice or saying a harsh word."

"Maybe you have a better man there than you thought."

"Yeah, I'm finding that out. Where is that barkeep? I definitely need a Siren's Potion!

"I think I'll join you. This has been quite a day!" Maurine signaled for the bartender.

———

Two hours later would find the ladies, joined by the men in the pod, gathered around the table, well on their way to their next hangover. The Siren's Potions were doing the job. And so far, dinner had not been served. Snacks, in the form of bowls of various nuts and spiced olives were strewn around on the table, but no serious food.

"You know what we need?" Al said. Profoundly. "We need some of that fish cooked up that we caught yesterday. Was it yesterday? Well, no matter. What are the chances of that, Maurine? Let's have a fish banquet! Cook it all, and we'll give fish to anybody that walks into the place."

"An excellent idea," Richard said.

"Yeah, I like that idea a lot!" James said enthusiastically.

And so, instructions were given, and the feast began. The cooks were as upbeat about it as everybody at the table. About half-way through dinner, James Harmon looked around the table and said, "Somebody is missing. Has anybody seen Chelsey?"

"Not since last night," Maurine said.

Everybody pulled up short and started looking at one another.

"She seemed happy enough at the beach party last

night," James said. "She was laughing and talking with those people from Oklahoma."

"Oh yeah," Richard said. "She was kinda warming up to that tall, lanky guy. I think he said he was from Oklahoma City."

"So maybe she got lucky!"

"It's possible. I mean, she is a grown woman. She's bound to be interested in *something* besides reporting!"

"Let's hear it for 'something besides reporting'," Al said, as he raised his glass high.

"Here, here!" Richard agreed and raised his glass. "Something besides reporting!"

And then everybody at the table raised their glasses, repeating the same thing.

James Harmon said, "Boy! I wish I had something in this glass besides soda for occasions like this."

"Soon enough, my boy! Soon enough," Al said.

"Let's take a momentary break from all of this jocularity," Angie said. "We need to talk about something serious for a moment, starting with a recap of the last several day's events. I hate to bring it up, but since I've been here, three people have been killed, a boat has been blown to smithereens; several of us have been involved in a suspicious plane crash. It was nothing short of a miracle that any of us survived that, by the way. Speaking of which, poor Niles didn't."

"And now, one of my guests might be missing," Maurine added.

"What?" Angie asked.

"I happen to know that the tall, lanky Oklahoman left this morning, on his way back home to Oklahoma. That pretty well knocks out the theory that Chelsey is shacked up with him, unless, that is, she fell in love and flew off to Oklahoma!"

Everybody suddenly got very quiet. "Is there a chance she could be with somebody else?"

"Anything is possible," Maurine said. "Possible, but not likely. Not unless the lady has round heels; and she doesn't appear to be that kind of person."

"We definitely need to check on that," Angie said. "Meanwhile, the elephant in the room is that we are sitting here without so much as a clue as to what we are doing. We need a plan. And I am in over my head this time. Richard, you had a security company for years. Your mind is bound to be geared for this kind of thing. We really need your help. *I* need your help."

"That puts us on the same page," Richard said rather somberly. "Because I have been thinking that very same thing ever since we got pulled out of that jungle. That bitch is spanking us, and one of the reasons why is because, up until now, we don't even know what she looks like! We're at more of a disadvantage than the Secret Service, protecting the President. They don't know who might come at him either. But at least they know exactly who the perp will be after.

"As things stand, we aren't sure where she will hit next. We don't know what she looks like. We aren't completely sure what weapon she will use. So, let's begin by examining her motive, or plural, 'motives' as it might be. First, like her sister, she wants to keep people away from the Blue Hole. Abducting Henry may or may not have had to do with that.

But killing the lady scuba diver couldn't have been anything else.

"Second is revenge against Angie and associates for taking out her sister. Revenge is a strong motive. But it has a flaw. Revenge is based on anger. And anytime a person or thing comes at you from anger, their thinking is clouded. No exceptions."

Angie and Scott looked at one another. Angie was thinking of Scott's cool demeanor when he had dropped the bomb on her earlier in the day about being aware of her infidelity. Scott, on the other hand, was thinking about Angie's fit of rage when she found out about his indiscretion. Which had been more effective, or for that matter, destructive? An interesting topic for discussion, perhaps in the next fifty years! For now, Richard was still detailing the problem at hand.

"Working on the basis of what we know, we could, 'under normal circumstances' second guess what she is going to do next. But these are not normal circumstances. She is not a human, she is some sort of mythological creature who's been around probably as long as her sister."

"A couple of thousand years," Angie offered.

"Yes. But she's bound to have an Achille's Heel. And chances are, it is very similar to the one her sister had. Angie, you had up front, close dealings with the sister. Tell me about her.

Angie interlocked her fingers and got a faraway look in her eyes. "Where do I begin? She had many vulnerabilities. First of all, she didn't really understand the thinking of the human mind. Her inexperience with humans worked against her. I totally befuddled her one time, out there on

Half-Moon Caye. She had lured Scott into the water and seduced him. Her plan was to get my goat, to make me furious with jealousy. When they came out of the water, I played it very cool and berated her for her efforts to take my man away. She came close to a melt-down."

Everybody laughed and took bites of food, or sips of their drink. Maurine slipped Dolly a bite of fish, which she had mashed, carefully, checking it for bones.

"Maris desperately wanted what she could never have. That was, in the final analysis, her undoing."

"What was that?" Richard asked.

"Love, marriage, a family, the normal things that most people want. It was unavailable to her because of who she was, because of what she was. She had never thought about that for two thousand years. But when Dimitri held a mirror up in front of her and made her see that, when the reality hit, it weakened her to the point of breaking her spirit."

"Fascinating," Maurine said. "It sounds like the elements of a poem. 'Even creatures of old seek the simplicity of love'."

"But love is never simple," Richard said. "It's the most complex of all emotions. To quote Star Trek, it goes where no man has gone before! In my life, I have seen the most emotionally unavailable, cold-eyed, cold hearted, mother's son, melt like butter in the sun when the right person came along."

"And, your point is?"

"Angie showed me the photo read-out on Scott's camera today. There was a woman, or at least a female figure standing over on the side, who had wings. To the naked eye, those wings were not visible. I believe that woman to be Maris's sister. What I'm not sure of is her motive for being there. Maybe, like her sister, she was doing a little recon, seeing who needed to be taken out and in what sequence.

"That was probably, indeed, her primary motive. But what she didn't want to admit to herself was a curiosity about humans. Maybe she wanted to see what it felt like to be standing around a fire on the beach, hearing happy voices sharing stories, laughing, smiling, feeling cama-raderie with each other. Let's take a guess at how much of that she gets in one hundred and fifty feet of water!"

"So, she's jealous of us?"

"You bet your ass she is! And I believe that to be our key to bringing this monster out of the closet. She's close to us. She's close to us right now. And my guess is, she wants in."

"So, like her sister, she wants to get to know us so that she can kill us?"

"Voila!" Richard said.

"Okay," Al said. "Where are you taking this? We were talking about a plan."

"The most vulnerable spy in the world is a spy who doesn't realize he's been exposed. We let her in, wait until we have her in the right place and position , then reverse her plan and put it to her."

"Sounds like a dangerous plan to me," Al said.

"If you come up with a better one, I'd be glad to listen to it," Richard said, but not sarcastically.

"No. I will bow to your experience and expertise. Besides, we just don't have that much to go on."

Scott, remembering that he had his camera, removed the lens cap and snapped a few pictures of the party around the table. Then laid his camera on the table, while he continued to stuff himself with snook.

"How can you eat any more?" Angie asked.

"I just love seafood," Scott said. "Actually, I've been full for a long time. But I just can't stop!" He placed another big bite of baked snook in his mouth and smiled, cheeks pooched out. Everybody was amused at that. But the food was delicious, so they understood Scott's over-indulgence.

Just at that moment, Chelsey came through the door, looking the worse for wear. She was wearing clean clothes, and fresh makeup. But her eyes said she was tired.

"Chelsey!" Angie said. "Where the hell have you been?"

Chelsey walked over to the table. She found a chair and dragged it near, between Angie and Maurine. Dolly immediately started growling. Chelsey looked down at her. "Oh dear! I'm afraid dogs don't like me very much. They never have." Chelsey got up and moved to the opposite side of the table. Then looked around and smiled.

"No," Maurine offered. "I think it has to do with the fact that I've been hand feeding her bits of fish. You got a little too close to the feeding ground. She's just being territorial."

"Well... I'm sorry if I worried you all. I'm afraid I disgraced myself with a bit of a debauch. Actually, his name was.. well.. it wouldn't be lady-like to tell. Let's just say that it was fun, but now it's done! Time to get back to being normal."

"If you're hungry, there's plenty of food," Maurine said. "Just help yourself. It was served family style tonight."

"Oh! Thank you," Chelsey said, looking at the food on the table. "Actually, I'm famished!" She picked up a plate and started placing pieces of food on it.

Angie looked at Richard. Sure enough, he was looking back at her, seeking Angie's eyes for a clue. Meanwhile, Chelsey had filled her plate and dug in like she was starving.

"So...let's talk about something else for a while," Richard suggested.

Angie looked over at Scott, trying to tell him something with her eyes, by looking first at him, then glancing at Chelsey, and back again. At first, Scott was confused as to what Angie wanted. But he finally got the message, leaned forward and eased his camera off of the table.

He lowered it down into his lap, turned it on, angled it in the direction where Chelsey was sitting and clicked the trigger. Afraid that she might hear multiple exposure clicks, he then placed the camera back on the table. He looked at Angie as if to say, "Got it," and went on with the conversation.

"I understand there are quite a few Mayan archaeological sites here in Belize," Richard said.

"Yes, there are," Maurine replied. "The Pre-Colombian Maya were all over Central America, from the Yucatan of Mexico, down to Honduras. Belize was certainly a part of that. We have three or four ancient lost cities here. But truth told, there are Mayan artifacts scattered all over our jungles. One gets the feeling they must have blanketed this region."

"At some point, I'd like to go on a road trip and visit a couple of those sites. I had quite an interest in them at one time, but never did anything about it. Now that I have been in close contact with some actual Maya Indians, I'd like to get to know more."

"Well, the pyramids in Belize aren't all that tall,"

Maurine said. "I think I can still climb them with you. I'd love to be your guide."

"Great!" Richard said with a smile. "Then let's plan on it."

"To the Maya!" Maurine said, raising her glass.

CHAPTER THIRTEEN

The Investigators

At first, Angie had suspected there might be something weird going on with Chelsey. But then she realized that was only because Dolly Dog had growled at her. Angie needed to be cautious to keep reasonable suspicions separate from paranoia. The line between those two things was as thin as a hair, and easy to cross over.

If fact, aside from seeming tired, Chelsey was her old self, laughing and chatting. Still, there was no definitive explanation for that lapse of time when she was missing. And the 'debauch' to which she had made reference, hadn't made an appearance with her. Why? Had it been a classic one night stand? Possible! Truth told, she didn't know Chelsey that well. Could that li'l ol' southern belle have a thing or two about her that stretched the envelope? 'That' was a strong possibility, Honey Bunch.

Meanwhile, Richard Hart was continuing to formulate a plan. But for some reason, he insisted on limiting the number of people who had access to his thoughts. And he had made it plain that Chelsey was not in the number. He had suspicions of his own.

So much so that he had a closed door meeting in Al and James Harmon's room to take possession of the obsidian dagger they had brought with them. He found a scabbard in the gift shop that the dark bladed knife fit into. From that moment forward, he carried the weapon on his belt at all times. Clearly, in Richard Hart's mind and heart, he was on maximum alert.

This did not slip past Maurine's radar. She was usually a fairly laid-back person, but she felt there was a tenseness in the air, and it concerned her. Everybody seemed to know that something was coming. They just didn't know in exactly what form it would come, or when. But one thing was for sure.. it was coming!

Scott and Angie seemed to be working on their relationship, taking walks, holding hands, doing a lot of talking. But even there, if body language meant anything at all, there was a gap. Was the infidelity on both of their parts really the issue? Or was that just the instrument that uncorked the wine?

———

Two very serious-looking men showed up at Robert's Grove, who displayed credentials identifying them as being investigators from the FAA. They were investigating the crash, and wanted to interview all four survivors, starting with Angie. There wasn't really a good place for a private meeting, so they settled for a table out on the deck, as far away from other resort guests as possible.

"We've been to the crash site, Ms. Holland," Strom Engel was saying. "It is a miracle that anybody walked away from that one alive."

"Yes it is," Angie said. Then, without thinking, she said, "I certainly don't think it was planned that way."

Both investigators were suddenly very alert. "What do you mean by that?" Strom asked.

Angie thought quickly. The truth but edited! "Something hit the side of the plane. It fucked up the controls. Niles saved us with his professional flying ability."

"Something hit the plane? That's the part we want to hear about. Do you know *what* hit the plane?"

"No. Never saw it. We were flying along normally. No issues. Then, there was this very loud banging sound, just behind the passenger seats that must have damaged the rutters, or something. Niles immediately started having problems trying to keep control of the aircraft."

"Did you see anything approaching the aircraft just before the impact?"

"No. Nothing. We were all talking. Everything was normal."

"Why were you up there?"

"A tourist flight. We wanted to see the Great Blue Hole and Lighthouse Reef from the air. Everything went smoothly. We flew out to the hole, did a couple of donuts around the hole, flew around the reef a little, took some pictures...we were on our way back."

The other investigator, Baron Jones, suspected something, but couldn't quite put his finger on it. "What is it that you are not telling us, Ms. Holland?"

"Nothing," Angie said, a little defensively. "What do you want, my bra size?"

"We have to ask..."

"Well, let me ask. What did you do with Niles?"

"He was extracted from the wreckage and the body sent to Belmopan for autopsy."

"Thank God for that. He deserves a decent burial."

"Yes Ma'am. His body will be turned over to his family for proper handling, just as soon as the autopsy is completed."

"I never understood that," Angie said, irritated. "Some poor bastard gets killed in a car wreck, or a plane crash, and then somebody wants to dice them up even more to figure out *why* they died. It's simple! Don't look now, but he was in a goddamned plane crash! He fucking died!" Angie was raising her voice and guests at other tables were looking at her.

She looked at the two investigators. "I've told you everything I know. This fucking interview is over. Who do you want to talk to next? I'll go get them for you."

"Uh, Richard Hart."

"Fine, wait your asses here. I'll fetch him. "What am I not telling you!" she muttered as she walked away. "Jeez! We were five thousand feet in the air. What do they think we were doing, playing volleyball?"

Angie found Richard in the reception office with Maurine and Dolly. He was signing employment papers and working out finite details regarding his responsibilities and compensation. The atmosphere was very pleasant and relaxed.

Angie walked up to the reception counter. "Deputy Dog

and his sidekick want to talk to you out there," she said as she pointed over her shoulder with her thumb.

"Okay," Richard said. Then he turned to Maurine. "Thank you. I'm beginning to feel like my feet are walking on solid ground again. I'm grateful to you, and to this lady over here (meaning Angie), for talking me into coming here instead of Ambergris Caye, then introducing me to you."

"Welcome aboard, Richard. It's exciting. You're going to be a wonderful addition to Robert's Grove," Maurine said. They shook hands and Richard left to go find the FAA Investigators. ".. and to me!" Maurine added, after Richard had walked out.

When Richard was well out of earshot, Angie looked at Maurine and said, "Congrats! What happened? I thought you two were going to wait until all of this crap was over with the situation at hand."

"Yes, well, I thought about that," Maurine said. "But I think I have done enough *waiting* in my life. There are several sayings about waiting, and none of them are good."

"What about, 'All good things come to those who wait'?"

"Yes, I know. But I like the one better that says, 'Fuck you. I don't want to wait!'"

Angie laughed. "Yeah, that is a better one!"

Meanwhile, out on the deck, Richard approached the two FAA Investigators, introduced himself, and sat down for his interview. It was almost a carbon copy of Angie's interview, even to the point of becoming irritated when Investigator Baron Jones suggested there was something Richard was not being up front about.

"You're looking in the wrong place for answers," Richard said. "We were victims. Do you think there is anything we would hide about a plane crash that almost got all of us killed? What school of investigation did you go to? You need to be out there at the crash site, going over that plane, or what's left of it, with a microscope. Go to your forensics. That's where your answers are."

"You talk like an investigator," Baron Jones remarked.

"I had my own security company for thirty years," Richard said. "And that was after I spent twelve years as a cop. Now, my opinion is, you two are a couple of Keystone Cop amateurs. I don't think you could find your dicks with a GPS. So, excuse me. I've got other things to do."

The rest of the afternoon went equally unwell for the two investigators. Even Chelsey, who showed what she was made of when pressed.

"What do you two guys think happened up there?" Chelsey asked.

"We ask the questions," Strom Engel said.

"Really? What kind of a deal is that?" Chelsey asked. "Pretty one-sided if you ask me. I mean, we were the ones up there that almost got killed. Now, you're sitting there telling me we don't have the right to some answers? I've got a message for you, and the horse you rode in on!"

With that, Chelsey pushed her chair back, stood up and stomped off. The two investigators packed up and left, rather non-plussed at their very limited productive session.

"I feel like we landed in the middle of a hornet's nest," Strom Engel said, as they got into their government car and drove away.

CHAPTER FOURTEEN

Lilly Meets Animus

Richard had never intended to get involved in some super-natural, mythological creature hunt. But here it was, and in a way, it was a blessing because he had been spiritually floating, without direction. Had no idea where he was going or what he wanted to do. All he knew was the pain of losing his precious Angela blinded anything that was put in front of him before now.

So, fate must have brought him here, to this place, in this time. Maybe the man up there had a plan for him after all. Or maybe Angela was sitting on his shoulder, gently guiding him. She always did try to steer him in the right direction. In any case, he was presented with a mission. And it was obvious that as dead set as Angie was on destroying the threat which was apparently Maris's sister, she didn't have any idea how to corner an enemy that refused to come at her straight on, like an honorable adversary. This one was like a sniper, attacking from a secret position. So, it was a good observation. How did the military deal with snipers? By fighting fire with fire. They had snipers of their own.

What they needed was a plan, something to poke the bitch in the ribs and make her lose her cool enough to expose herself. But without information to work with, that was going to be tough. "Tough, maybe," Richard mused, but not impossible. A plan was hatching in Richard's mind!

That afternoon, Richard had a closed meeting with Maurine, Angie, Al and James. Not even Chelsey was privy to what Richard was planning. Maurine got on the computer and ordered a very special 'prop' that would be needed for the plan. Three days passed while the crew waited impatiently. Then, the package arrived. After inspecting it closely, they prepared it via use of the air compressor, then made sure the bathing suit and hat were the right size. After all preparations were made, they immediately headed for The Great Blue Hole.

They had to obtain special permits to gain access to the Blue Hole. The Belize Coast Guard had it blocked off to all traffic. But Maurine called a friend of hers who worked for the Belize Government, and he pulled strings, especially after Maurine explained what she had in mind. She also provided the sixty-foot Dorado for their plan. The Dorado; the dive boat belonging to Robert's Grove Resort that is outfitted for that purpose exclusively. It would be an easily identifiable target.

Once on site at The Great Blue Hole, everybody geared up to dive. But before they did that, they needed to stretch the tarp over the stern for a couple of minutes, while they completed one other task. When that was done, they removed the tarp.

They appeared to be in a party mood, laughing and joking and making comments about how exciting it was going to be to see the grottos again. Once they were geared up, they sat on the gunwale, Richard gave the signal, and they all fell backward, into the water. They checked their equipment for the last time, making sure their air pressure was correct, then purged their BCs and sank beneath the surface. They gathered together on the sandy slope, gave thumbs up, and went over the edge into the Blue Hole. From there, they drifted straight down.

But at one hundred feet, they quit descending. Instead, they moved their fins slowly to and fro, and held steady. They did not go through the thermocline. Richard gave the signal, and they began to slowly surface.

There was no need for a decompression stop, as they had not gone deep enough, nor had they stayed long enough. Instead, they immediately surfaced and found James Harmon waiting on the dive platform for them.

Angie was the first one to climb up the ladder, out of the water. "Well," she said, with anticipation. "Were we successful? Did it work?"

"Like a solid gold charm!" James said, smiling from ear to ear. James told his story, even while the other divers managed to climb out of the water and into the stern of the yacht.

"Charles (the boat captain), and I hid in the lounge. Both of us had our cell phones set to 'video'. So, it was all very quick! I mean, like lightning! That bitch swooped down out of nowhere and grabbed Lilly with fucking *huge* talons. When she did, Lilly sort of exploded, with a 'Boom!' And let me tell you, *THAT* pissed her off! She made this real loud screeching sound and flew almost straight up before she took off toward the south. Then she dropped what was left of poor Lilly in the water, over there," James pointed.

Richard nodded approval. "Never wanted one of those inflatable sex dolls before today. Now, I think we've found the perfect use for one! So, we've managed to get her goat. Let us hope this is the beginning of her undoing!

"Can you imagine what she must have thought when she believed she was going to nail her next victim, and instead, got a face full of hot air," Al said, smiling. Everyone then laughed. Richard looked at the boat captain. "Let's go home, Charles. Mission accomplished.

As the Dorado steered its way through the coral heads, leaving the Blue Hole, a strange creature peeked out from behind a protruding coral head less than a half mile away from them. This creature had the head, arms and breasts of a beautiful woman, but her bottom half was covered with feathers. She had muscular legs, like an extremely large bird of prey, each armed with large, razor sharp talons. Finally, she had large wings, which she moved back and forth, slowly. The expression on her face as she watched the retreating boat was one of unbridled fury. She glared at these retreating humans through almond-shaped eyes, with elliptical pupils. These inferior humans thought they could trifle with her and get away with it? She would prove them wrong and make them regret their folly. After all, her name was Animus!

Aboard the Dorado, everyone was in the salon, gathered around James' cell phone, looking at the footage he had captured of the creature attacking the inflatable sex doll. James had not exaggerated; the attack had been swift. His video footage lasted less than five seconds. But it was revealing enough! The creature that had attacked the doll was like nothing any of them had ever seen. It/she was definitely not of this world, or, as reported, she was a creature straight from the pages of mythology. Richard couldn't believe his eyes.

"Sweet Jesus," he said. "I never realized what a sheltered life I had lived. I mean, I studied mythology in school, but like everybody else, I took it with a grain of salt. Never in my wildest imagination did I lend it any credence! I always thought, as everyone else did, that it was the Greek version of parables. Most stories based in mythology seem to be based on various morals or talk about taboos. Uh, like Oedipus. Killed his father, married his mother, then poked his eyes out when he realized the truth. Definitely a treatise prohibiting incest. Even Pandora, broke the rules and opened her box. All of her blessings escaped except hope; things like that.

"But now...over two thousand years later, we're discovering that those poor bastards were basing their stories on living gods and demons? How did Shakespeare put it? 'There are more things in Heaven and Earth, Horatio, than are dreamt of in your philosophy.'"

"That being the case," Angie said, softly, "it would appear that you, like me, have been chosen by somebody that is a lot wiser than us, to be the ones who battle these creatures."

Richard looked up at Angie. "Yes, so it would seem!" For some reason, the droning of the diesel engines seemed louder as everyone in the salon sank deep into their own reverie.

———

Back at Robert's Grove, Maurine waited on the dock as the Dorado came in for a slow motion docking. She had an expectant look on her face. "How did it go out there?" she asked.

"Textbook," Richard said, as he stepped from the boat to the dock, following Angie. "She took the bait just as I planned. Now, the next move is hers. You can believe right now she is fuming. So it won't be long. Her next move is going to be based on getting even, to teach us a lesson, to not mess with her."

"What do you think she will do?" Maurine asked.

"I don't have a clue," Richard admitted. "But we need to keep an eye out, because my guess is, she is coming, and she is going to be pissed when she does."

Meanwhile, at that precise moment, at Lighthouse Reef, Animus sat atop an exposed coral head, one elbow on her knee, her chin in her hand. What could she do to teach these inferior humans a lesson? She would ponder this until she formulated the perfect plan. She had never been treated so disrespectfully. There must be recompense. No such insult should go unpunished!

CHAPTER FIFTEEN

The Lightning Rods

R ichard had fallen into a very pensive mood. He sat at a table in the restaurant, drinking a cold beer and looking out the window. Maurine walked in with Dolly at her side and joined him.

"What gives?" she asked.

"I'm thinking about all of the mysteries in this world," Richard said. "All of my life I have lived in a little box of my own making. I mean, I thought I was a pretty well rounded guy. Then, in the past few days, I have been shown something that I would have never believed existed, if I hadn't seen it for myself. I am just in awe. That's all."

"It seems to be affecting you rather deeply," Maurine observed.

Richard chuckled. "I'm a little surprised at that myself. There was a time in my life when I kept almost everything out. After all, I was a macho, gun toting para-cop who operated a business where I hired other gun toting para-cops. You have to put on a certain façade when you hold a position like that."

"Were you happy, being that person?"

"I never thought about it that much. I was successful, keeping the bills paid, that's all that mattered. I'm just now beginning to realize that there was a lot I was missing. Things that were right in front of me."

"Example?"

"I see you with your little dog. It's obvious that she loves you. It is also obvious that you love her. You give her lots of attention. The two of you are close. I had a dog. He would wag his tail when I came home from work. I would pat him on the head, say some little thing to him. But I never really knew him. One day, he died. I let the vet dispose of the body. Never thought about it, except for how much the vet bill was. I don't think you would have liked that Richard. Thinking back, I sure don't."

"What does that have to do with the situation at hand?"

"Nothing," Richard said. "But when you open a door, all sorts of things come into sight. Not just the one thing you are looking for."

"Do you mind an observation?"

"Not at all. Wha-cha got?"

"It seems to me like you're having an epiphany. That isn't all that unusual. But you need to lighten up on yourself a little. You're worried about not appreciating things 'then' the way you do now. But Richard, that part is natural too. You don't quit growing just because you turn twenty-one. You'll continue to evolve every day of your life. Maybe you've just been pushing it away or hiding it from yourself."

Richard didn't look at Maurine, but he was definitely processing what she had just told him. "Interesting insight," he finally said. "Thank you. I think you and I are going to be very good friends."

"I hope so. I'd like that," she said, and smiled. "Who knows, one of these days, you might even find love again."

Richard looked at his drink and smiled a half smile. "Well, nothing is impossible, but I really doubt that will happen."

"Why not?" Maurine asked.

"Well, I'm just not looking for that. Good friends, yeah. Romance, no. Maybe in a few years, but certainly no time soon."

This was not what Maurine wanted to hear. But, oh well. At least Richard would be here, working. So, who knew what feelings might develop? Maurine needed something to hug, so she reached down and picked up Dolly. It was a beautiful evening. For now, that was enough.

———

Chelsey, in a lounge chair, on the deck by the swimming pool, grabbed her cell phone, which she kept in her tote bag and looked for a special new number she had stored there. She hit the call button and waited.

"Jake? Chelsey. Surprise! ... Well, I just miss you a little and wanted to hear your voice. Are you all the way back in Oklahoma?..... Ha ha! What? What's that sound in the background? It sounds like kids playing. Where are you? ... What?... Oh my God, Jake! You never told me that! You should have told me! Married? And just how many kids, Jake? Oh, my God! Oh my God!.... No, I certainly won't! You never have to worry about hearing from me again, you

cheating sonofabitch! God! You used me! You lowlife....
Hello?"

Tears filled Chelsey's eyes as she hit the 'END' button.
"Bastard!" she said out loud. Then went to the bar to get a
Siren's Potion. "Make it strong," she said.

———

Out on the beach, James and Al Harmon stood, looking out
at the water, and to the north, where the sky was turning
dark blue. Lightning could be seen playing in the clouds.

"Looks like we're going to get some more wet stuff," Al
said.

"Yeah," James agreed. "I like the storms down here. You
ever notice how the thunder is different here than it is at
home?"

"What do you mean?"

"Well, I like to call it stereo thunder. The thunder will
start off in the clouds way in the distance, then roll across
the sky until it's right over the top of you, then fade off into
the distance. It's really neat!"

"That's called rolling thunder. And yeah, it does seem to
be more common here than in Texas."

Just then, they heard footsteps behind them and looked
up to see Chelsey approaching with a drink in her hand.
She also had tears in her eyes.

"Hey there, Gal! What you up to?"

"I'm gonna get drunker than Cooter Brown," she
responded.

"Oh?" Al said. "Any particular reason why do you want
to do that?"

"Because I found out that son of a bitch from Oklahoma doesn't have a surrey with the fringe on top. He has a wife and a house full of kids! A little detail he failed to mention while he was pulling my panties down."

"Would it have made any difference?" Al asked.

"Of course it would have!" Chelsey protested. "Do I look like a slut to you? God! He used me! All I was, was a one-night stand. A vessel for him to put his pecker in! Dirty bastard!" Chelsey took a deep pull on the straw, dropping the level in her glass at least an inch. She wiped her tears away with the back of her hand. "Ah well, fuck it! Lesson learned," she said. "I think I'll go for a walk on the beach."

She started walking with the open water to her left. "I wouldn't go too far if I were you," Al warned. "That storm looks like it's moving in pretty fast!"

"Yeah, yeah, okay," she said over her shoulder. "Maybe if I get wet enough, it will wash away my sins!" With that, Chelsey walked away, sucking on her drink. Her body language indicated absolute frustration.

In their room, Angie and Scott 'fiddled.' Under normal circumstances, Scott would be slipping his arms around Angie and pulling her close to him with more than smooching on his mind. But something was in the air.

Suddenly, and without warning, Angie said, "I don't feel close to you anymore, Scott."

Scott could not have been more stunned if you had caught his head in between two cymbals.

"What?"

"I'm sorry. I love you. I'm just not 'in' love with you."

"Oh my God! Angie! I do love you. And I need you. I wouldn't know what to do without you. Can't we discuss this?"

"Sure. We can discuss it all you want. I owe you that much. But the fact is, the magic is gone. Well, truth told, I'm not sure there ever was actual 'magic' per se. But I am no longer in awe of you. It doesn't feel special to be with you, or around you. It used to be, when we walked into a room together and I was holding onto your arm, I felt like everybody in the room was looking at us and saying 'Wow'. I don't feel like that anymore.

"Because?"

"Well, first you screwed Maris in some kind of an underwater 'do me'. I forgave you for that because I understood the hypnotic ability of that vixen from hell. But then you banged the cowgirl on the King Ranch. And now I'm wondering if you might have tapped something when you were on assignment in Africa. Did you, Scott? Was there some little 'indiscretion' while you were taking pictures of birds?"

Scott stood silent and motionless next to the bed. Angie watched him closely, then nodded her head. "I see. So, tell me, how many times did you drill for pussy juice on that trip?"

"You're telling it. What difference does it make what the truth is? This will be the second plane crash we've been in during this trip. So, go ahead. Imagine anything you want!"

"Are you denying cheating on me in Africa?"

"Oh, *now* you're asking me? Yes, I deny it. There's nothing to deny! All I did was work. Work and think about you. I couldn't wait to get through with the assignment so I could get back over here to you. I was worried sick about you, and with good cause, I might add. As usual, you had your ass hanging out on a limb. You know, instead of all this imaginary fornication, what we really need to talk about is this penchant of yours for diddling around with these extremely dangerous goddamned ancient whatevers! This is Belize. It ain't our problem! Let the Belizeans figure it out. Huh? What about that shit? Now there's a very real, up front problem! So tell me, are you really worried about me sticking my weenie in something besides you? Or are you on a fishing expedition, trying to find something to be pissed off at me about?"

By now, the normally composed Scott Carrington was coming unglued. He was shouting, pacing around the room, gesticulating.

"Let's do a little recap of the past several days' events here, and oh, feel free to stop me anytime you think I have misspoken. San Leon, Texas: You get a weed up your ass because you 'have a gut feeling that something' is fixing to happen. Eh? Right so far? So, because of that weed, you jump on a plane and fly to goddamned Belize where, during the flight, you meet some ham bone retiree named Richard Hart, who should be named Richard the Lion Hearted because, and I will give you this one, he is a brave sonofabitch. Of course, he might also be crazy as a shit house rat, because he goes around wearing a goddamned knife on his belt twenty-four seven. But what the hell, he hasn't committed mass murder yet, so we're good... so far.

"Meanwhile, people are dying, getting their guts eat out. And we, including Richard the Lion Hearted, are in a fucking plane crash, where somebody else gets killed. We do the hokey pokey with a bunch of Maya Indians in the middle of the frigging jungle until you 'just happen' to remember that, Oh, shit! You've got your cell phone with you! Now, please allow me to skip to the good part..."

"There's a good part?" Angie says in defeat.

"Oh yes. We don't want to leave out the best part of all. Things aren't insane enough, so you go poking the tiger with a sharp stick! You and Richard order a suck/fuck blow up doll because Richard has had a brain fart about how to piss off the monster a little more. Right? And we go to the trouble to water all the way out to the Blue Hole for the sole purpose of springing our trap. It works! The bitch takes the bait! Now, you can believe, she's got the red ass and is doing her best to plan how to kill more of us! Nice work!

"But...this cake would not be complete without the icing. I come rushing down here because I am worried out of my mind about your recklessness. I love you, so I keep my trap shut and support you all that I can. Now, your way of thanking me for my dedication and caring is to drag me through the cactus... no! Cut my heart out and hand it to me, because I got a little too plowed in cowboy land and diddled a cowgirl. And yes, that was wrong. I admit it. It was bad. I feel awful that it happened. And it might be unforgivable, except for the fact that you did worse with some Greek named Dimitri, who was apparently hung like a mule. Then, to add to your indiscretion, you got three sheets to the wind and bragged about the size of his pecker to a bunch of *reporters* out there on the deck in front of the restaurant! *Reporters*, Angie! Reporters!

"How am I doing so far? So, bringing us to the current

situation, you want to break up with me because... I am apparently unworthy of your love and trust and fidelity, which in your estimation is as pure as the driven snow? Let me know if I've left any important parts out!

"In synopsis, here is the way I see it, and oh, I promise to keep this as short as possible. Then I'll shut up and you can pound me with a sledgehammer for a while, just in case you haven't inflicted enough pain on my heart for your satisfaction. We make a good team. Both of us are flawed, yes. But we still make a damn good team. I take pictures, you sell those pictures. We both make a good living at it. I love you, I thought you loved me. We have a good life; beach house, small fishing boat, dog, barbeque pit, friends, neighbors. True, it isn't a non-stop party. We don't dance naked in the fountain every night. We don't even have a fountain, for that matter.

"What we do have is something millions of people wish they had... a *normal* life! Home cooked meals, a wide screen TV, cars in the driveway that are less than two years old, cell phones, computers, a king-sized bed! *We don't need this shit down here, Angie!* Let's go home! Let's go back to our normal, hum-drum, undramatic lives where the big issue of the day is that a seagull did a fly-by and crapped on the deck! Huh? I want that life, not all this, God forsaken, bullshit drama with two thousand year old beings. Fuck 'em!

"You know, I might be able to handle all of this a little while longer, but now you're standing there telling me we might be near the end? I can't handle that! Why don't you just shoot me and get it over with? I'm lost without you. Call me weak, co-dependent, whatever the fuck you want to call me. But I can't imagine a life without you. Okay. I'll stop. Your turn!"

Angie sat in her chair, silent for several minutes. At last, "I don't know what I was thinking. Everything you said was crystalline truth. Please... just forget my stupid outburst."

"Come on," Scott said. "Let's go to the Cantina Del Robert's Grove and get smashed!"

"Together!" Angie said, with a meek smiled.

———

The dark clouds were moving closer in. On the beach, Al and James Harmon started walking toward the resort, abandoning their spot on the beach.

"You know, Dad," James said. "The last time we had a thunder-storm like this, lightning apparently hit Oscar's boat and blew it to hell."

"Yeah, that was weird. But Maurine told me his insurance company is going to replace the boat. At least that's good news."

"Yeah, but that isn't where I'm going with this."

"No? Okay, where are you going?"

"This creature... Maris's sister. She can fly. Do you think she somehow uses the low clouds to her advantage?"

"Interesting thought. But I don't know how she could do that. She would have to be able to manipulate nature."

"No. Not so much manipulate as, take advantage of, use for her own purposes."

"Sort of, 'ride the storm' if you will."

"Yeah, it's just a thought. What if she placed something

on top of Oscar's boat that night that actually attracted the lightning?"

"Something akin to a lightning rod? I suppose it's possible."

"Working on that theory, she doesn't want people going to the Blue Hole. She can't kill everybody... let's hope. So, the next best thing is to eliminate the vehicles that take people to the Blue Hole."

"So, the Dorado would be her next target!"

"Bingo!"

"We've got to move fast, James!" Al said, as they fairly ran toward the restaurant to find Richard and tell him of their misgivings.

It didn't take long to explain what they predicted was going to happen with the approaching thunder-storm. What they said made sense to Richard, who went into action, showing cool professionalism and quick thinking.

Within minutes, he had put together a couple of workers, assembled tools and materials to manufacture a couple of make-shift lightning rods, which they secured atop the Dorado's cabin with strong deck screws, and ran the cables to ground on the outer side of the dock. The rain started pattering down just as he and his men completed their task.

"There," Richard said. "I don't know what that creepy creature has in mind, but I hope this befuddles it!" With that, the crew sought shelter against the rain.

They didn't have long to wait, to find out if their prediction would come true. A little while later, as they sat in the restaurant, eating supper and chatting lightly, there was a horrendous boom. Lightning had hit somewhere close. Richard had located an umbrella, just for this possibility.

With umbrella in hand, Richard and Maurine walked outside to a point where they could see the Dorado. It was unscathed. Just at that moment, they heard an awful screeching sound that was reminiscent of an extremely large bird of prey, or maybe screeching brakes on a train.

And then they saw her. She was about a hundred feet off of the ground, above the Dorado, looking down at the failure of her attempt to destroy this vessel. And even from here, it was obvious that she was livid, furious. This human was making a fool of her. He would be her next target! She would teach this inferior human a lesson that he would never forget…in hell!

Then, Animus flapped her wings in fury and flew away. Maurine and Richard stood there, in the rain, looking at the Dorado.

"You saved my boat," she said.

"No," Richard said. "James and Al Harmon saved your boat. They're the ones that figured out what that thing was going to do. All I did was act on their prediction. I think we both need to go thank them."

They didn't have far to go. James, Al, Angie and Scott were all standing in the rain, gawking in awe at the accuracy of their prediction. When they were near, Maurine placed her hands on James' shoulders and kissed him on the cheek. "You are an amazing genius," she said. "Come on, let's all get out of this rain.

In the restaurant, Maurine had the cooks prepare a pate made of lobster that was incredibly delicious. All parties present, ate, drank and laughed at outfoxing the creature. Then, Richard said somberly, "She will come at us again, for certain. It's not even a matter of if, but when and where.

My prediction is, it will be soon, because now, after failing two times in a row, she is really pissed. She screeched out there tonight, and it was like a sound from the center of the earth."

"Yeah, she's got her panties in a twist, for sure," James said. "She will come. We have to be ready for anything."

Maurine looked around the table, smiling. "I am surrounded by some amazing people. I am in awe of all of you. I just want you to know how grateful I am to every one of you."

They all raised their glasses to that, as the party continued.

"We had better enjoy it while we can," James Harmon said. "Cause something bad is coming. I can feel it."

CHAPTER SIXTEEN

The Last Flight of Animus

It was the following morning. The rain had abated, and everybody was standing on the dock beside the Dorado, trying to see what, if any, damage the lightning bolt had done. But Richard and crew had done a good job. The insulted coating was burned off of the cables. But aside from that, there was no discernable damage.

"Thank God," Maurine said. Then she placed her arm around Richard's waist and was pleasantly surprised when he reciprocated by putting his arm around her waist. It felt good to her, warm and secure. She was so glad this man had been brought into her life. This first indication that he cared for her would grow into something beautiful, she just knew it would. She could sense it. All she needed to do was be patient, not push him. It was clear that he needed love in his life, and she was willing to offer that.

James Harmon, standing in the stern of the yacht, said, "Can you imagine what this boat would have looked like if Richard hadn't Jerry rigged those lightning rods!"

"Yeah, I can," Al said. "It would be part two of the Belize What You Want."

"Heaven help us," Scott said. Everyone thought he was talking about the boat. But when they looked up to see what he was looking at in the distance, they refocused to see Chelsey, walking toward them, still in her yesterday clothes, soaking wet. She looked drawn, exhausted.

"Jesus Christ," Angie said. "He was a one-night stand! Did she really go off the deep end over him? When Chelsey got closer, she slowed and came to a stop.

"Hello, everybody," she said rather meekly.

Everybody returned the greeting. "You look like refried dog shit," Angie said. "Let me help you back to your room. You need a warm bath, and to get out of those wet clothes."

"No. I'm alright. I'll go in a minute," she said. She was still carrying her glass from the previous evening. But Angie noticed it still had liquid in it. It was water, and Angie had a flash that it was not fresh water, but rather, salt water, necessary for survival of sea creatures. Just at that moment, Chelsey took a sip of the water through her straw. Angie made her way over to Richard and said something to him, very softly.

In turn, Richard, very casually, meandered over toward Chelsey and worked his way behind her.

"Well, we were all worried about you," Angie said. "We're all glad you are alright."

Maurine was picking up on something suspicious in the air, but at first, she couldn't figure out what it was. James, on the other hand, sensed it right away. So did Scott and Al.

"So...how's your Kappa Kappa?" Angie asked.

"I'm sorry. My what? Kappa? I don't understand."

"What have you done with Chelsey?" Angie suddenly demanded. "Goddammit! What have you done with her?"

All of a sudden, the person that was supposedly Chelsey changed into a different being before everybody's eyes. A strange looking woman stood there with weird, piercing almond-shaped eyes that had elliptical pupils. She did not look human. Her top half was woman-like. But the bottom half of her bore feathers, and muscular bird legs armed with huge, razor sharp talons. Finally, wings began to appear.

"Chelsey is dead," Animus hissed, "just as all of you will be!"

"Why do you want to kill us?" James Harmon asked.

"Because you killed my sister. And because you rape, and take and take, and take. In return, you foul the earth with your refuse and pollution. You kill each other. You're killing this earth, and don't even care! Now we need to start killing you."

"Good luck with that," Richard said, as he quickly wrapped one arm around the neck of Animus. But the creature was stronger than he anticipated, and she shrugged him off, causing him to lurch backward and fall to the ground. It was clear that she was about to take flight. So, Richard quickly jumped up and wrapped his arm around her neck a second time. But this time he used a special maneuver he knew, which locked his grip on her, and made it near impossible for her to break loose from him a second time.

In her fury, she screeched a horrible, furious sound, spread her wings, flapped them and rose from the ground, flying straight upward. Richard hung on for dear life. At first, he had to use both arms to make sure he stayed with her, such was the speed and G force of her ascent. But a few seconds later, he managed to adjust to her upward thrust, wrapped his legs around her torso. He then summoned all of his strength and determination to unsnap the safety strap on the scabbard which held the obsidian dagger. Pulling the dark blade from the scabbard, Richard almost lost his grip on the weapon. But then he regained a firm hold on it and managed to position it so that he could plunge it into her back at a place close to where the heart would be on a normal being.

Animus shrieked a terrifying cry of pain, did corkscrews in the air as she ascended higher, trying to free herself from Richard Hart. But he was strong for his age and resolved to dispatch this creature from hell. He pulled the blade out, then plunged it in again, in a slightly different spot. Again, the creature shrieked a terrible cry from the piercing pain.

In an effort to shake Richard loose from her, she rolled over and briefly flew on her back. She was almost success-ful. Richard began to lose his grip. But she was unsuccess-ful. Richard stayed with her by tightening his legs around her even more. In this way, he was also able to get a more firm grip on the handle of the dagger and make sure it didn't work its way out. In fact, he managed to twist the dagger until he felt Animus weaken. She no longer had the strength to maintain flight. Her wings finally stopped beat-ing, over five hundred feet from the ground. Without the power of her wings, she plummeted toward earth.

The last words Richard ever said, as he plunged to the ground, holding on to Animus were, "Angela, I'm coming!"

Then, there was a terrible crash as Animus and Richard

hit the ground. Animus' bleeding body began to morph. There, before everyone's eyes, she slowly turned from flesh to ashes, just as her sister had done. Richard laid there, dead, but at peace. Those who saw his crushed and broken body remarked that it looked like he had a smile on his face.

———

One year later, a beachcomber, looking for seashells on the beach at Manuel Antonio/Quepos, on the south coast of Costa Rica, came upon a beautiful blonde woman, standing barefoot on the sand, looking out at the sea.

"Pura Vida!" he said to her, smiling broadly.

"Pura Vida, yourself," the woman said.

"My name is Carlos," the beachcomber said, and extended his hand in greeting.

The woman accepted his hand. "Angie," she said.

"Americana?" Carlos asked.

"Yes," she said.

"Great! What brings you to our beautiful country?" Carlos asked.

"I'm not sure," Angie replied. "Just... an instinct. A premonition."

ABOUT THE AUTHOR

GEORGE DISMUKES spent the first half of his life in pursuit of adventure. This ranged from bullfighting as a youth to milking poisonous snakes professionally at Ross Allen's Reptile Institute in Silver Springs, Florida. The early 60s found him pursuing wild animals across the Serengeti in the movie business and operating an animal export company in Iquitos, Peru. He spent many years exploring archaeological sites of the ancient Maya Indians in Central America and studying their lost civilization. He also lived in Honduras, where the story, TWO FACES OF THE JAGUAR, THE LOST CITY, and THE JAGUAR'S QUEST take place.

In 1980, he began a video production company in Houston, Texas and worked as a 'triple threat' (writer/director/producer) creating some of the Houston market's most creative television commercials. He won a CLEO award for his production of a series of television PSAs concerning prevention of child abuse, funded through a grant from the University of Houston.

Currently, he lives on the Texas Coast with his soul mate and closest friend, Nadine, where he writes and works in magazine advertising. His hobbies include growing exotic chili peppers and experimenting with salsa recipes. Above all, George is a devout animal lover and advocate, fighting against animal abuse. He has two dogs, named Pulga and Gizmo, respectively.

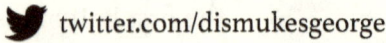 twitter.com/dismukesgeorge

ALSO BY GEORGE DISMUKES

Two Faces of the Jaguar Series

Two Faces of the Jaguar

The Lost City, Two Faces of the Jaguar

The Jaguar's Quest

Siren Song Series

Siren Song

Siren Song II

Siren Hunter